The Amanda Staples Series

The Amanda Staples series is a paranormal series of short stories written by Australian author A.A.G. Sharp. The stories are set-in present-day Melbourne, Australia, and follow Amanda, as she comes to terms with getting glimpses of the future, and trying to understand their purpose and meaning.

BASAL PRESS

Details about Basal Press and contact information can be found at the website: www.basalpress.com

A catalogue record for this book is available from the National Library of Australia

ISBN 978 0 64568 880 1

Basal Press acknowledges that Aboriginal and Torres Strait Islander people are the Traditional Owners and the first storytellers of the land on which we live. Basal Press recognises their continuing connection to the Land, Water and Culture and we pay our respects to their Elders: past, present and emerging.

Psychic Phantasm

The Amanda Staples Series

By

A.A.G. Sharp

BASAL PRESS

Table of Contents

Snapped Vision

A Knock to the Head

Amanda was being examined by her doctor. "I feel so silly. I was trying to catch my phone and hit my head on the desk."

"Well, a knock to the head needs to be checked out. It's good you came in. I've just completed some simple concussion tests. All seems okay, vision, balance, and reflexes. I recommend you take it easy over the next couple of days. Don't overexert yourself and get some good sleep. Even consider taking tomorrow off." The doctor shifted back to her desk.

"Come on Jane. You know I run my own business, and I hardly get a chance to take time off." She was a world-renowned expert in Emotional Intelligence. With her success came an ever-increasing inbox of requests from clients, and a largely self-inflicted expectation to continue pioneering growth in the field. The initial novelty of being able to work flexibly and remotely was now somewhat of a burden.

"I'm your doctor and that's what I recommend." Jane raised an eyebrow and glared at Amanda.

"I know, but tomorrow my assistant is coming in to go over preparations for a Canberra conference I'm attending next week." Amanda put her jacket back on and sat next to her doctor. She raised her hand to her temple feeling for a bump. She felt nothing unusual.

"You may get a bruise on your head. Oh, I've been meaning to ask. Are you still getting those Ocular Migraines?"

"Yes, I'm trying to spend less time in front of a screen and when they happen, I just rest my eyes for five to ten minutes and they go away." Amanda had been suffering them more than she wanted to let on to her doctor.

"If they become more intense or more frequent, come and see me. Try drinking less coffee." They both laughed at the suggestion. The consultation was over, Amanda collected her things and said goodbye.

Amanda's townhouse was within walking distance of the medical clinic. She had called her doctor's clinic from her office and had been lucky to get an appointment as it was late afternoon. Once she explained she had hit her head, the receptionist managed to squeeze her in. Amanda had come straight home after knocking her head to rest before she headed off to see her doctor. When Amanda returned to her townhouse, she was greeted by her playful 3-year-old miniature Schnauzer, Sassy.

"Hello, beautiful. Told you I wouldn't be long." She reached down and gave Sassy a scratch behind the ear. She swayed a bit as she stood up. "Wow. I'd better go and sit down. Come on." Sassy scampered along the hall, in front of Amanda, which led into an open plan kitchen and lounge room. Amanda put her things on the kitchen bench and slumped into her favourite chair. Sassy jumped straight onto her lap. Amanda closed her eyes and just tried to relax as she patted her dog.

"Damn, my phone." Amanda pushed Sassy off her lap. Slowly she stood up and retrieved her mobile out of her handbag. Back in the chair, she investigated the damage.

"Well, looks like this has had it. Badly cracked screen. Chip out of the top corner. Not good." Amanda was talking to Sassy. She tried turning her mobile on again and nothing happened. "Tomorrow morning, I will just have to buy myself a new phone. I must admit I do fancy one of those new smartphones." Sassy was staring up at her owner, head slightly to one side as if trying to understand what she was saying.

"I'd better feed you and think about my own dinner." Amanda stood up and headed for the kitchen. Sassy was hot on her heels.

A New Phone

Amanda Staples was 44, currently single and an early riser. Her morning routine included a short walk with Sassy. Then a 5km run, with a friend, followed by a fruit smoothy. Her office was in Melbourne's CBD and it only took her about fifteen minutes by tram from her townhouse in Middle Park. She would grab her morning skinny latte from the coffee shop in Little Collins Street and be in her office by 7:45 am. Business was thriving, she travelled all over the world delivering her Emotional Intelligence courses and consulting to large companies. She had been invited to deliver a paper at a national conference being held in Canberra next week on the Tuesday.

Her assistant, Megan Wheeler, came in one or two days a week. It was Wednesday and Amanda expected Megan in around 9 am, after dropping her daughter off at daycare.

"Hi. Did you get my message?" Megan called out as she dropped her things at the reception desk.

"No. You wouldn't believe it; I smashed my phone." Amanda looked up from her desk as Megan poked her head in. "It's a write off."

"Oh! What did you do to your head?" Megan came into the office.

"Is it that noticeable?" Amanda raised her hand to her forehead. Still no bump. "I thought I had applied enough makeup."

"It looks like a smudge."

"Oh. Great! I hope it's gone by next week." Amanda was thinking about the conference.

"That's what my message was about." Megan sat in a chair opposite Amanda. "I had to change your bookings. Sorry, but now you fly up on Monday night. I booked you into the Guest apartments. The airline said there was some mix-up or double booking. They cancelled your morning flight."

"Damn. I will have to get someone at short notice to look after Sassy."

"I can drop in and feed her. Will she be okay overnight?"

"Yes, I suppose so. Thanks." Amanda picked up her broken phone. "I need a new one. Now you are here, I'll pop down to the local retailer."

"What are you going to get?"

"Same brand, I guess." Amanda stood up, grabbed her handbag, and headed for the front door. Megan headed back to the reception desk.

Amanda was disappointed when the shop assistant told her they had sold out of the latest phone in her band. When Amanda commented she really wanted to stay with the same brand, the assistant offered an alternative - remembering the manager had suggested that they should sell their demo model. If a customer didn't mind that the packaging had been opened, they would sell it at a discount. Amanda agreed to have a look. The assistant went out back and returned with the phone in hand and a charging cable. It appeared to be the latest model.

The young shop assistant was all over the features of the new smartphone. Dual camera, Super Slow-Mo, and infinity display to name a few. "This revolutionary camera adapts like the human eye because of the dual aperture. The Super Slow-Mo is really cool. 960 frames per second." The assistant was in his element, but Amanda had tuned out. All she wanted was to sign the contract and get back to her office. Another ten minutes later and after a Slow-Mo demo, Amanda finally got a word in. "Yes. I'll buy it."

It took another ten minutes for the assistant to work his magic and transfer the data from her old phone to the new one, sign a contract and leave the shop. Amanda was back on the grid. Immediately her phone started going off with all the messages and notifications that had been waiting for her to come back on-line.

Back in her office, Amanda spent the rest of the morning catching up and replying to messages. The afternoon was spent working with Megan reviewing and editing her presentation for Canberra.

"Good luck. See you next week." It was 4:30 pm and Megan was off to collect her daughter.

"Bye." Amanda spent the next half hour dealing with her emails. She liked to leave at the end of the day having read, replied and filed all the day's emails. Quite an achievement on some days.

Phantasms

Just before Amanda left her office, she picked up her new phone and downloaded her favourite Apps. When she had finished, she tried to remember what the shop assistant had said about Slow-Mo videos. It was all a bit confusing, so she grabbed her things and left her office.

Amanda headed down Collins Street towards King Street. It was a lovely early spring afternoon, and the sun was shining down through the trees. She thought back to her phone and pulled it out of her handbag. '*I'm in no hurry, I'll practice taking a video.*' She thought as she heard a tram coming down Collins, heading towards Southern Cross train station. Amanda positioned herself on the kerb and started the video as the tram past in front of her. It was approaching the King Street intersection.

To her shock, she videoed a man running across in front of the tram and he was struck. The tram slammed on the brakes, sounded its horn but all to no avail. The man was knocked several metres onto the ground. The video stopped just after the point of impact. Amanda looked up from her phone at the scene in front of her. The tram was still moving and in fact, had now past through the intersection. She did a quick search of the intersection. There was no man on the road. People were going about their business as nothing had happened.

Amanda double-checked her phone. Instead of a video, she was looking at a still snapshot of a man lying on the ground in front of the stationary tram. She couldn't believe it. She looked at the intersection again. Everything was fine. Cars and pedestrians crossing as usual. She pressed the Home button on the screen. She would have a look at the picture more closely once she got home. She was feeling a little bit rattled, but she put her phone away and headed for her tram stop.

Amanda opened her door. "Hello, beautiful. Guess what happened to me?" Sassy jumped in excitement but that was more at seeing her owner.

"I got a new phone." Amanda pulled it out of her handbag and showed Sassy. Amanda continued into the lounge and sat in her favourite chair. Sassy wanted to jump on Amanda's lap, but her owner stopped her. "No. You can sit there for a moment. I want to look at my phone."

Amanda opened her gallery to look at the last thing she had taken.

"What! Where's it gone?" She was looking at a short video of a tram passing by. There was no accident and no man. She played the video over and over. She searched through her gallery. Nothing. No record of the accident she thought she had recorded on her phone. Amanda couldn't believe it. Was her mind playing tricks on her?

Amanda was interrupted by Sassy nuzzling her leg.

"Sorry, Sassy. I suppose you want to be fed?" Amanda placed her phone on the side table and went to the kitchen. After giving Sassy her dinner, Amanda switched on the TV to watch the news.

"A man was hit and killed by a tram at the intersection of Collins and King Streets this evening. Both streets have been blocked off by police and there is now traffic gridlock in the city." The newsreader continued to Amanda's disbelieve. "Our reporter on the scene is Michelle Taylor. Michelle, can you tell us the latest?"

The reporter was standing almost exactly on the spot Amanda had taken the video. A stationary tram was visible in the background. "Police say a man in his forties was struck at about 6:40 pm as he tried to run across the intersection. He died at the scene. The roads will be blocked to traffic for at least two hours as police investigate the accident. Back to you Colin."

Amanda dashed to her phone and opened the gallery. The video was the same. No accident. There was no image of the man. She slumped into her chair dumbfounded.

The phone rang, and Amanda jumped. She looked at the screen and saw the caller ID was Jenni, her closest friend. Jenni was a similar age to Amanda. She worked as a solicitor with a large law firm and was divorced with no kids.

"Hi Amanda. Just calling to confirm tickets for Saturday's races." The cheery voice of Jenni brought Amanda back to reality.

"Hi. You won't believe what has happened to me."

"Are you okay? Do you want me to come over?" Jenni expressed her concern.

"I'm okay, just a weird thing happening with my new phone. Would be great to see you though, can you pop by tomorrow?"

"Sure. I can make time in the afternoon. I'll come to your office." Jenni was intrigued. "At least give me a hint?"

"No, it will be easier face to face." Amanda changed the topic. "So, we're going to the races?"

"Yes. We've got tickets into the Black Caviar Restaurant. A colleague of mine managed to pull some strings. Three tickets for you, me and Margo." Jenni sounded excited.

"Sounds great. Gotta go. I haven't had dinner yet and I'm starving." Amanda's stomach was grumbling.

"See you tomorrow then, for the big reveal. Ciao." Jenni laughed and they hung up.

Amanda thought back. *'What time did I take the video?'* She opened the gallery on her phone and checked the details of the video. The timestamp was 5:42 pm. Almost an hour before the news reporter said the accident occurred.

"That's interesting." Amanda said as she headed for the kitchen. Her mind was racing as she prepared her dinner.

Next morning, Amanda was working on her new book. By mid-morning she needed a coffee and headed for her usual café. Phone in hand, she decided to try another video. She was in Little Collins Street near a pedestrian crossing. She pointed the camera up the hill and started the video. No traffic was on the road. Then she videoed a cyclist coming towards her. A person in a car didn't look and opened their door. The cyclist slammed into the open door ending up on the road. The video stopped just after the impact, quickly Amanda looked up at the road. No cyclist. The car was there and there was a person sitting in it. Amanda was puzzled. Last time she had actually seen a tram go past, even though it wasn't the tram in the accident. She looked at her phone again. Once again there was no video, just a snapshot of the cyclist laying on the road after hitting the car door. She looked up again and to her surprise, the cyclist was now actually coming along the road.

Amanda immediately waved and yelled out, but it was too late. The person in the car opened the door. Amanda pressed the home button put her phone in her pocket and ran to help the cyclist.

"Are you okay."

The person from the car was also there. "I'm sorry. I didn't see him." He tried to explain. The cyclist slowly got to his feet and looked at his bike. He seemed to be okay. No major injuries. He looked at Amanda. "Why did you wave at me?"

"I was trying to warn you. I could see this man was about to exit his car." She replied.

"Thanks, but no thanks. You distracted me. I could have avoided him." The cyclist picked up his damaged bike and walked off the road.

"I'm sorry." Said Amanda aghast. She didn't know what to do. So, she headed back to her office, leaving the man from the car and the cyclist talking about their insurance.

Back in her office, Amanda pulled her phone out and once again opened the gallery. Sure enough, the video was there. No photo of the accident. Just a video of an empty street. She was so frustrated. She had no evidence. No one would believe her.

This time the vision had happened only minutes before the accident. Not like the man killed by the tram. Amanda thought, '*Am I going mad?*' She sat pondering this question for some time.

Race Day

Jenni and Margo were already seated at a table when Amanda arrived.

"Hi. Sorry, I'm late. I missed my train." Amanda gave both her friends a peck on the cheek before sitting at the table. "This is all a bit swish." She commented about the Restaurant.

"I told you it would be good," Jenni replied.

"What's this about your new phone? Jenni said you're having troubles with it or something." Margo asked.

Jenni interrupted. "I only said that something weird was going on with your new phone. I told Margo she should wait and hear the whole story from you." Jenni smiled at Amanda.

"Well, as I explained to Jenni, I think I have been seeing visions." Amanda was a bit coy.

"Don't be ridiculous. You had a knock on the head. You're imagining things." Margo was not buying into any visions. Amanda and Jenni both looked at each other and laughed. That was typical Margo. Margo was Amanda's publicist and friend since Amanda published her first book, nine years ago. She was a number of years older an Amanda, married to husband Frank, and they had one grown up son, Micheal.

"It's weird how the video changes into a snapshot of the incident, but when I return to look at it in the gallery, it's a video without any record of the incident." Amanda was trying to explain to her friends as best she could.

"So, no proof." Exclaimed Jenni.

"Correct." Amanda was interrupted by the waiter. It was time to order drinks.

The afternoon went by with the friends chatting about all manner of things. They placed a few small bets on the odd race without much success.

The second to last race of the day was coming up and Jenni made a suggestion. "I've got an idea. How about we put your phone to a test?"

"What do you suggest?" Amanda had forgotten about her phone during the course of the afternoon.

"Video the finish of this race and see what happens." Jenni smiled.

"You're going to pander to this notion of visions?" Margo was sceptical.

"Why not? It might give Amanda some answers."

"Okay. I'll do it." Amanda agreed.

Amanda and her friends positioned themselves in the seats overlooking the track. They were right near the finishing post. The race was 1200 metres and as the horses rounded the bend and entered the straight, Amanda started the video. The horses were about 300 metres from the finish and charging home under the whip. Jenni and Margo were watching the race, but Amanda was watching her screen. The horses flashed by. The video stopped on its own as the winner was crossing the line. She didn't notice anything odd and certainly, there was no incident or accident like before.

"Well, what did you see?" Jenni was enthusiastic. She glanced over at Amanda's phone.

"Look, the video has changed into a snapshot of the finish line with the first three horses in the frame." Amanda excitedly showed her friends. Margo who had placed a bet and picked the winner immediately noticed something odd. "That's not the winner. I picked the winner, it was number 7, Ice Lady."

They all had a closer look at the phone. The winning horse had a number 3 on the saddle cloth. Jenni immediately looked at her racebook. She had recorded all the winner so far for the day.

"No horse with the number 3 has won a race today." She explained to her friends.

"What numbers are on the placegetters?" Asked Margo.

"Ah. Second has the number 9 and the third looks like the number 1. It could be number 10, hard to tell." Amanda had zoomed in on the horses.

"Well, I can confirm that those are not the numbers of the placegetters in this race." Margo pointed to the large screen displaying the results of the last race.

"Hey. I've got an idea. Let's look at the next race. See how many horses are in it." Jenni was getting more excited.

Margo and Jenni both opened their race books to the last race for the day.

"There are only nine horses." They said in unison.

"Let's place a bet on the last. A trifecta with horses 3, 9 and 1. What do you say?" Jenni smiled.

"Do you really think that snapshot is a vision of the winners of the next race?" Margo ever the doubter.

"It might prove I'm not imagining things," Amanda commented.

The three agreed. Jenni suggested pooling $10 each and she headed off to place the bet.

They sat silently watching as the horses left the mounting yard and headed for the starting gates for the last race. Before the race started, Amanda had exited her camera and gone back into the gallery. Sure enough, the video was there. The snapshot of the winners had gone.

The light was flashing, then the horses jumped. The friends were all on the edge of their seats. As the horses rounded the bend, the race caller had number 1 out in front. Number 9 was in the middle of the field and number 3 was coming last. Their hearts sank.

Suddenly, Jenni jumped out of her seat. "Look, number 3 is making a run."

Number 3 had already passed two horses and there was still 250 metres to go. Number 3 caught up to number 9 and together they started passing all the other horses. Then it was only number 1 in front. When they hit the finish line it was 3, 9 and 1 just as the snapshot had predicted. The friends went wild.

The trifecta paid just over $2,700. Amanda felt guilty keeping the winnings, so Margo came up with a compromise. "Let's keep enough money to cover our tickets and lunch for today, the rest you can donate to charity."

"I think that's fair." Agreed Jenni.

"Okay, now do you both believe me? I'm not going mad." Amanda was anxiously looking for support.

"Yes, we believe you." They answered in unison. Both had smiles on their faces.

"What do you intend to do with this new power of yours?" Asked Margo.

"I don't know." Amanda was still unsure what the visions meant. What was their purpose?

A Terror Hoax

The Canberra conference was at Old Parliament House. Amanda had arrived the night before. Her presentation was the last session of the day. She hated the prospect of being last. During the lunch break, she decided to go out for a walk and some fresh air to clear her head. She was still puzzled by the visions. Nothing had happened since the races. In a way, she was hoping it was over.

She headed toward new Parliament House. Amanda thought, *'I'll give it one more go. See if it is still happening.'* She was standing on the East side, near the entrance to Parliament House. There was hardly anyone about. Amanda pulled out her phone. She looked at the entrance and started the video. Her attention was suddenly drawn to a sound off camera, it was a car screeching to a halt. She turned her phone towards the sound.

To her horror, she videoed a white van on the kerb. Three dark-clad figures jumped out and ran for the entrance. They were armed with what looked like semi-automatic assault rifles. They started shooting at the security guards and stormed the front entrance. The video stopped as they burst through the entrance.

Amanda quickly surveyed the scene in front of her. To her relief, there was no van, no attackers. The security guards were still standing in their positions unhurt. She looked at her phone. It clearly showed three dark-clad figures entering the building, shooting their weapons. Two security guards were lying on the ground seemingly dead.

Panic set in. '*What do I do? When will the attack happen?*' Amanda started to think about whether she should approach the security guards to warn them of a potential attack. Next, she is running toward Parliament House. Heart racing, at the main entrance, she asks to see someone in charge.

"Why?" A guard asked.

"I have potential information regarding an imminent attack on Parliament House."

The security guard quickly ushered Amanda through the entrance and got the attention of her superior.

"Sir. This lady would like a word."

"Okay. Put your things through the security scanner and then come with me." Sergeant Philips instructed Amanda. She reluctantly placed her handbag and phone in a tray provided and watched nervously as they went through the scanner. She went through the security screen and picked up her things. The Sergeant ushered her into an interview room.

"How can I help you?" Philips asked as he shut the door.

Amanda sat in the chair provided and braced herself. "I think there will be an attack on the parliament."

"What sort of attack are you talking about?"

She had gotten his attention. "Three people with assault rifles."

"How do you know this is going to happen?"

"Hard to explain. Can I speak to the person in charge of security?" Amanda was gaining in confidence.

"I'll call them. What's your name?" He dialled someone on his mobile.

"Amanda Staples. I'm from Melbourne."

Sergeant Philips spoke to someone and then hung up. "While we wait. When is the attack going to happen?"

"I don't know. Here, have a look at this." Amanda showed Philips the picture on her phone.

Amanda warned the Sergeant. "Whatever you do, don't exit the picture. We will lose it if you do. It needs to stay on the screen." Philips studied the picture. He zoomed in on the attackers and the security guards.

"When did you take this?"

"Just before I came to see you."

"But there has been no attack."

"As I said, it's hard to explain."

The door opened and a serious-looking man entered. He was wearing a normal business suit.

"I'm Commander Williams. What's this about an attack?"

"This is Ms Amanda Staples. She has this on her phone."

Amanda nervously added. "Careful. Don't swipe it or exit from the picture. You will lose it."

"When did you take this?" Asked the Commander as he studied the picture.

"In the last 15 minutes. Just before I came to see the Sergeant."

"Is this some sort of hoax? What are you after?" The Commander was angry.

"It's no hoax. I've been having visions through my phone. This is not the first. I video the vision and it snaps a picture. The actual event happens sometime later. Usually within an hour or so. So, you need to do something now about getting ready for an attack." Amanda had an urgency in her voice.

"Where are you from? Why are you here?" The Commander was glaring at her.

"I'm from Melbourne and I'm attending a conference at Old Parliament House. This is wasting time."

"What do you think?" The Commander turned to the Sergeant.

"It's unusual. Maybe, to be on the safe side, we should call for reinforcements."

"That would mean locking down parliament as well. HQ won't send reinforcements without raising the alert level. They'll want a reason." The Commander was hesitant.

"A tip-off. An anonymous caller. A bomb threat." The Sergeant shrugged his shoulders.

"Okay." Finally, the Commander agreed. "I'll call and ask for the terrorist response team. I'll tell them we have had an anonymous threat of an imminent terrorist attack. You go an inform the guards out front. Bring them inside, lock the doors and issue weapons. Then issue a 'lockdown' alarm for the house." The Commander glared at Amanda. "If this is a hoax. You are going to be in big trouble." He started dialling a number on his phone.

This is not a Drill

Sirens sounded. "Whoop, Whoop ..."

A voice announced. "This is an emergency lockdown. Do not evacuate the building. Stay put and wait for further instructions. This is not a drill. I repeat this is not a drill." The "Whoops" continued.

The Commander said. "You will have to stay here. I'll send in a guard and take your phone." Amanda tried to object. The Commander insisted and then left with the phone.

Soon a junior officer entered the room. "What's happening?" Amanda asked.

"It's crazy out there. People are running all over the place. The Assistant Secretary of Security Branch is demanding answers."

"No attack then?" Amanda's heart sank.

"Nothing."

An hour passed and then another. No attack. The Commander entered the room with another man.

"Ms Staples, this is William Petersham, Assistant Secretary of Security Branch."

"Ms Staples, you are in serious trouble. I have asked the AFP to charge you under the Terrorism Act. Do you know how much disruption you have caused?"

"Oh! I'm sorry. I had a vision, and I don't know when it will happen, but my experience so far, is that it will happen soon." Amanda was nearly in tears.

"So, you're sticking to your story. Let me look at the picture again."

The Commander produced the phone. "Can you enter your pin? Please."

Amanda obliged. Surprisingly, the photo was still open on the phone. The Assistant Secretary studied the picture. "It looks real. How did you doctor it up?"

"I didn't." Amanda was adamant.

"Commander Williams says you are here for a conference. What's the conference about?"

"Emotional Intelligence. I was meant to present a paper this afternoon. Too late now."

"And this was at Old Parliament House? What were you doing out the front of here?" Petersham was pushy.

"Stretching my legs. It was the lunchtime break."

"I don't know your motives, but I'm sure the AFP will find something. Are you part of a group?" Petersham asked.

"No. I came to warn you of an attack. You can see in the picture. Two of your officers get shot. I thought it was pretty important to warn someone."

"Okay." Petersham was dismissive. "Do you have accommodation for the night?"

"No. I have a flight booked for 6:40 pm back to Melbourne."

"Well, you won't be going on that. The AFP will have to organise a place for you to stay overnight. You'll be appearing in court tomorrow." The Assistant Secretary left.

Much later, Amanda was eventually escorted to a local hotel for the night. After a restless night, Amanda was having a late breakfast in her room, watching the morning news.

The main headline of the morning had been; "A terror hoax at parliament house disrupts question time and the rest of the days sitting. A middle-aged woman is being held for questioning by the AFP."

Suddenly, there was breaking news. "We interrupt this bulletin. There is an incident currently taking place at Parliament House. Gunshots have been heard. We are now crossing live to our chief political reporter, Tony Myers."

The screen flashed to somewhere outside Parliament House. "Tony. What can you report?"

"Sally, there has been a shootout between AFP officers, and we think three terrorists. The AFP is reporting that the terrorists have been shot and two killed. There seems to be no casualties on the AFP side. A press conference has been scheduled for 12 noon, when the AFP Commissioner will brief the media."

"Thanks, Tony. We have to leave it there. More on the terror attack after the break. When we will return live to Parliament House." Amanda jumped as her phone rang.

"Commander Williams here. Looks like you were right."

"I just heard the news. They said no AFP casualties. How come the two officers in my picture didn't get shot?"

"I took some precautions. Much to my boss's displeasure. I posted a couple of snipers on the roof and had the guards wear extra protection. We remained on full alert into this morning."

"I'm glad none of your men got hurt. Am I in the clear?" Amanda asked.

"Well, I imagine you won't be charged, but someone will want to examine that phone of yours more closely. You've still got a lot of questions to answer. I've got to go. Thanks for warning us." He hung up.

Amanda pondered. *'Why am I getting these visions?'*

Surveillance 101

The Aftermath

It was all over the news and Amanda's friends wanted to know everything about her Canberra adventure. Luckily, Amanda didn't have her phone, otherwise it would be constantly going off. The AFP had kept Amanda's phone for testing. When she first returned from Canberra, she had purchased herself a basic phone and blocked the caller ID. She wanted to remain anonymous and didn't want people contacting her just yet. Especially the press. This gave Amanda a small window of a day or two, where no one could harass her over the phone. Even her friends had to wait until they got together face to face. Amanda felt it would be easier telling her friends about the dramatic events in person.

Amanda was seated at a table right in the back of the restaurant. She had asked for somewhere quiet and the waiter had directed her to that table, at which she now waited for her friends. Jenni was the first to arrive. She was gushing as ever and the two warmly embraced and then sat down. "Oh my god, Amanda. What an ordeal? Are you okay?"

"I'm fine. Yes, it was pretty full-on." Amanda was still trying to come to terms with what had happened. Had her phone actually predicted a terror attack on Parliament House?

"Did they arrest you?"

"No. Just held me for questioning." Amanda held up her hand to stop Jenni's questioning.

"Hang on a moment, let's wait until Margo gets here. I don't want to go over this twice." Amanda studied the menu giving Jenni a hint, she needed to wait a little longer.

Margo arrived a little out of breath. "I had to run to dodge the rain. You been here long?" Margo asked Jenni as she settled into her seat.

"No. I just arrived. Amanda, can we get started now?" Jenni was impatient.

"Oh, yes. Amanda how are you coping? It must have been shocking." Margo remembered why they were there.

Amanda cleared her throat. "How about we all make an order, then I will fill you in on my adventure." She gave her friends a wry smile. Reluctantly, Jenni agreed.

The waiter confirmed their orders and filled their glasses with water before leaving them alone to chat. It was unusual for them to only have water filling their glasses. Margo was a bit puzzled as to why.

"Okay. No alcohol, I don't want any hysterics." Her friends both glanced at each other.

"I'll start at the beginning, but please try not to interrupt me. First of all, don't believe everything you've heard on the news. They are stretching the truth a bit. Anyway, during the day, I got bored with the conference and decided I needed a break. Some fresh air. So, I walked up the hill towards Parliament House. I don't know why, but I started videoing around the front of the building. The next thing I know, my phone is recording this van pulling up. The doors were flung open and three black-clad individuals, exit the van and race towards the main entrance with guns blazing."

"Did you hear all the sounds, as they are happening on your screen?" Margo asked.

"Yes. It's like it really is happening. I heard the guns firing, the screams from the guards and bullets flying past."

"You must have been terrified." Margo commented. Amanda paused as the waiter returned with their meals. Once the waiter had left their table, Amanda continued.

"Well, yes, but of course it wasn't happening right then. It was happening in the future and displaying on my phone." She spent the next two hours narrating the rest of the story and answering the avalanche of questions. Her two friends were particularly interested in the AFP's response to Amanda's warning.

"So, this Commander Williams, half-believed you?" Margo asked.

"I suppose so. He did place snipers on the roof." Amanda confirmed.

"And they let you go?" Margo expressed a note of surprise.

"Yes, but as I mentioned, I had to stay overnight. Things erupted the next morning."

"Now what happens?" Jenni was intrigued.

"Well, they have my phone. Not sure when I will get it back. I have a temporary replacement." Amanda picked up the small basic phone to show her friends.

"You blocked the caller ID. I didn't know it was you when you called the other day." Margo was a bit upset that perhaps Amanda didn't trust her.

"I'm sorry, but I really don't want this number getting out. Commander Williams warned me that the press will try anything to contact me."

Jenni commented. "It's amazing they haven't discovered your address."

"Yes. Well luckily, the conference organisers didn't ask for my home or work address details. They only had my post office box for correspondence, besides everything is done by email these days. Also, the AFP only told the press I was a visiting speaker from Melbourne." Amanda sounded relieved.

"But you're a well-known author and Emotional Intelligence consultant. Surely, they could go to the conference website or just go on social media and find something." Jenni was puzzled.

Margo interrupted. "Well, I made sure Amanda's publisher didn't let anything get out about her or her address."

"Thanks, Margo. I know the press has been hounding them. And Jenni, perhaps I'm a little more careful than some in what I put on social media. So far, I've been lucky, I guess." Amanda raised her eyebrows at Jenni.

"Will there be anything more?" The waiter surprised them.

"No. Thank you. We are finished." Amanda confirmed. Her friends were a little miffed as they wanted more, but Amanda said she was tied. So, the friends said goodbye and Amanda promised to keep them informed of any future news. She added that they should catch up again next week. Jenni agreed to arrange it.

A Job Offer

The next day Amanda's phone arrived by special courier. She opened the package and studied her phone. Everything looked in order. She decided at that moment to refrain from using the video on her phone ever again. Videoing the future was a bit unnerving. She immediately called her two friends and told them she had her phone back.

Shortly after Amanda had finished talking to Margo, her mobile rang. She was in her office reviewing notes for a new podcast she was developing. Her phone had been amazingly quiet since its return. Amanda looked at the caller ID and was surprised to see the name, Phillip Williams.

"Hello." She answered the phone a bit uncertain.

"Hi, Amanda. It's Phil Williams from the AFP."

"Did you enter your number in my contacts?" Amanda was surprised, but relieved now she knew it was Commander Williams.

"Sorry. I just thought you might want to know it was me calling, given the circumstances. It would give you a chance to ignore me, if you wanted to."

Amanda pondered his response before continuing. "Did you get anything from my phone?"

"Nothing. There was a basic video of Parliament House and nothing else. It is just an ordinary phone." He sounded disappointed.

Amanda was sort of relieved. "Does this mean the investigation is now over?"

"Not exactly. I'm not really involved in the actual investigation. I know they are still following some leads and are still trying to work out a motive for the attack." Amanda got the feeling he didn't want to elaborate any further.

"Is there anything else you wanted to talk to me about?" She cringed after asking, as she thought she would have rather finish the phone call.

"Well. Yes, there is actually." Williams paused before continuing. "I've had a transfer, and I now work in the Diplomatic Service section of the AFP. At my own discretion, I can hire consultants to assist in our investigations."

Amanda was thinking. '*Where is he heading with this?*'

"I would like to hire you and your phone. What do you say?" The Commander waited.

"My phone?" Amanda was dumbstruck.

"Yes. I think we need to do some experiments and see if you and your phone really can predict the future or was it something else. I'm on a plane tonight flying to Melbourne. Let's discuss this over lunch. See you tomorrow. Bye." He hung up before she could say no.

"The nerve." Amanda glared at the caller ID on her phone, before noticing Megan, her assistant, was standing at the door. "Are you alright?"

"I don't know. I think I've just had a job offer." Amanda half-smiled.

Surveillance

A man in his mid-forties and bordering on good looking, pushed the door open and approached the reception desk.

"Hello. I'm Phil Williams. I'm here to see Amanda Staples."

Megan smiled and nodded. "Please, have a seat and I'll let her know you're here." She quickly dashed to Amanda's office. Once inside she hastily closed the door. "He's here." She blurted out. "He's rather handsome." She added with a smile.

"Damn. I was really hoping he wouldn't show." Amanda paused. "Tell him I'll be out in a minute."

Megan opened the door and returned to her desk. "Amanda will be out shortly. Can I get you some water?" She tried to appear calm.

"No. Thank you. We will be going straight out to lunch." He said confidently.

Amanda stood up. Straightened her dress and put on her jacket. She put her mobile in the jacket pocket, grabbed her handbag and walked calmly out to meet the AFP Commander.

She approached him with her hand extended. "Hello, Commander Williams."

"Please, call me Phil. No need for formalities." He stood up and shook her hand warmly. "Nice to meet you again. Are you ready to go?"

"Sure." Amanda turned to Megan. "Please close up for me. I'll see you next week." She then indicated to Phil; she was ready. He opened the door for her. "Goodbye." He nodded to Megan as he followed Amanda out the door.

The restaurant was a couple of blocks from Amanda's office. They walked there in relative silence.

"Can I get you some drinks before you order?" The waiter hovered around as they settled into their seats.

"Amanda. What would you like?"

"What are you having?" She would let him make the choice.

"I'll have a Pinot Grigio."

"The same, thanks." The waiter nodded and left them to study the menu.

"So, what is it exactly you want me to do?" Amanda came straight to the point.

"Simple surveillance. As I mentioned, I now work in the Diplomatic Service, and we have a foreign diplomat that's of interest to us. We have been keeping an eye on him for some time."

"What?" Amanda was surprised.

"Please, let me explain." Phil sat back as the waiter poured their wine. After they made their lunch orders and the waiter had left, Phil continued.

"I want to test that phone of yours and I think I have an opportunity. A French diplomat is having an affair with a Public Servant in the Defence Department. You do know that the Australian Government is working with the French on Australia's next submarines?" He presumed she had heard something.

"I have seen something about it on the news."

"Well, the French contract is reaching a major decision point, and some changes might be on the cards. We just want to make sure they don't get any inside information."

"You think this diplomat may be grooming the Public Servant, in order to gain information." Amanda was starting to gain interest.

"Exactly. We have had them both under surveillance for a while. So far, it looks like an innocent affair. But a key date is coming up and I was wondering. If you and your phone really can see the future, I would like to try it out on this couple and see if anything materialises."

"That's a big stretch. I've only captured four events on my phone, and they have all been random." Amanda was sceptical. "I can't control what happens on the screen. It's a mystery."

"The more we test your phone the more you may discover. Wouldn't you like that?" Phil was appealing to her curiosity. "If you could control it in some way. Imagine the possibilities."

"I have been racking my brain about how and why this is happening. It is bugging me. A test might provide answers." She pondered what could happened.

"Treat it like a controlled experiment and see what happens." He was feeling more confident now, that Amanda would agree.

Amanda hesitated to gather her thoughts. Phil studied her but remain quiet.

"Okay. What do I need to do?" She tentatively agreed.

"Thank you." Phil was relieved. "We know when the couple meet. Usually in public places, so there is nothing seedy. We will put you in position, at the place we know they are about to meet. Then all I need you to do is use your phone to video them and let's see what your phone records."

"So, I just hold up my phone and point it at this couple. Isn't that a bit creepy. Won't they get suspicious?" Amanda was starting to reconsider.

"No. You'll be fine. We have some experts that will show you the ropes." Phil gave her a big smile.

Under Cover

"Is this meant to be a disguise?" Amanda was looking at herself in a mirror. She was wearing a plain white blouse and dark slacks. But it was the large floppy hat and big sunglasses she was wondering about.

"No. It's not a disguise." Replied a female AFP officer, who had been helping Amanda select clothes and prepare for her first assignment. "We just want you to blend in with the crowd. Others around you will be wearing something similar."

Phil Williams had contacted Amanda, and they were ready to test her phone. He had given her instructions on where to go and who she would be meeting. The AFP officer, helping Amanda, adjusted the hat one last time. Then the officers phone rang. She listened to the caller, and then hung up. "It's time we got you into position." She informed Amanda.

The two left the apartment they had been using and headed for the foyer. The restaurant fronted the Yarra River on Southbank. The AFP officer directed Amanda to a table, and they were joined by another male officer. Amanda faced the river while the two officers faced

Amanda effectively shielding her from tables at the front of the restaurant and the promenade along the river.

"How long do we have to wait?" Amanda nervously asked.

"Five to ten minutes." The female officer replied. "Position your phone on the table as we have practised and get ready to record."

Amanda did as she was told. The camera was on, ready to record. She waited for the signal. The male AFP officer touched his hand to his ear. Listening to the incoming instructions then signalled Amanda to start recording.

She pressed record. Her hands were shaking a bit, so she took a deep breath and tried to calm herself. Her phone was pointing at a couple of tables near the front. Amanda had no idea what the target couple looked like. She waited, concentrating on her screen.

A man walked into the picture and sat down on his own at one of the tables. A waiter served him and then left. Then a couple appeared, and they sat at the table next to the single man. They were obviously a couple and leaned in towards each other smiling. Another man appeared next. He was carrying an envelope that looked rather fat. He sat down at the table with the single man. They exchanged a few words. The new arrival passed the envelope under the table to the other man, then he stood up and left. Amanda suddenly realised the video had stopped. The screen was clearly showing a snapshot of the two men exchanging the envelope. Amanda started to panic.

"Sorry, but the video has stopped." Amanda nervously whispered to the AFP officers. One of them looked over his shoulder at the couple. They were now being served their lunch. He turned back and told Amanda. "Start videoing again. They are still there."

Amanda protested. "But, if I do that, the image I've recorded will be lost."

The female AFP officer immediately pulled out her phone and dialled Commander Williams. "We have a situation. The phone has stopped recording."

"What's Amanda say?"

"She said, the snapshot will be lost, if she starts videoing again. What do you want us to do?"

"Tell Amanda not to touch her phone. Wait for the couple to go, contact me again, then I will join you." Phil hung up.

Amanda looked up at the single man. He had not moved and there was no sign of the other man or the fat envelope.

Reviewing the Evidence

Amanda and Phil were back in the hotel apartment. Phil was studying a laptop and Amanda's phone was lying next to it. She was looking over his shoulder. "So, you were also videoing them on another camera?" She asked.

"Yes, plus we had the table bugged. That way we could hear their conversation. You were too far away for your phone to record what they were saying." He adjusted the laptop screen. A video was playing. "There they are. The couple has just arrived at their table. Look. There is your man." Phil pointed at the edge of the video.

Amanda could see the single man seated on his own just in view of the camera. They watched in silence for what seemed like ages. Eventually, both the couple and the single man left. Phil stopped the play back of the video. No one had joined the man and there was certainly no passing of an envelope.

Phil looked at the still photo on Amanda's phone again. It showed both men's faces clearly, and the envelope being passed under the table.

"What happens now?" Amanda asked.

"We have left our hidden camera in place at the restaurant and changed its angle slightly to focus on that table." He pointed at Amanda's image. "If your phone has recorded the future. At some point, that man will return, his friend will appear and hand over that envelope." He once again indicated on the screen.

"What's in it and who are those men?"

"Money, I presume. I have arranged for their faces to be run through our databases to see if we have a match. Hopefully, we will get a match and I'll be able to answer your questions."

"Sorry, my phone didn't uncover anything about your couple." Amanda, a bit disappointed, moved over and sat on a lounge chair.

"That's okay. As you said, you can't control what happens on the screen. Have you videoed anything else since you got your phone back?" Phil was curious.

"No. To be honest, I'm a little scared of what I might see."

"I suppose that's understandable." Phil closed the laptop and stood up. He picked up Amanda's phone and gave it to her. "Thank you. I'll let you know if we get a match or if anything develops. I connected you phone to my laptop and surprisingly managed to get a copy of the image. So, you can exit the photo now." He then indicated that she could go. "Goodbye, I'll wait to hear from you then." Amanda smiled and walked out of the apartment.

A Chance Rescue

Amanda left the building and walked along the Yarra River heading for the Queens Bridge to cross back to her office. She was thinking, *'I'm an Emotional Intelligence expert, I shouldn't be scared of what I might video.'* So, while she was walking, she pulled out her phone and pointed it along the river and started the video. A woman appeared standing on the edge of the river. She was just admiring the view of Melbourne and the river. Then Amanda noticed a teenager on a skateboard rapidly approaching from the other direction. The skateboard must have hit something, and the teenager was thrown forward off the board and stumbled straight into the woman. The impact sent her headlong toward the river. The video stopped at the point of impact.

Amanda quickly looked up from her phone. To her surprise, the woman was standing a short way in front of her, at the side of the river. Amanda approached her but was hesitant to say anything. Not knowing how she was going to warn her. She eventually stopped next to the woman and spoke to her.

"Nice view, isn't it?" The woman turned and smiled. Just then Amanda caught sight of the skateboarder, in the corner of her eye, heading their way. Amanda reached out and grabbed the woman's arm and pulled her out of the way, just as the skateboarder came tumbling off the board. "Watch out!" Amanda exclaimed and the woman screamed.

The skateboarder luckily, came to a halt at the edge of the river. He got up, dusted himself off, picked up his board and walked away. The woman was horrified. "He could have knocked me into the river."

Amanda asked. "Are you alright?"

"Yes, thank you. I can't swim. I could have drowned." The woman was still in a state of shock. She took a couple deep breathes and then turned to Amanda. "Lucky you saw him coming. Thank you, so much."

"Come and sit down." Amanda guided the woman to one of the seats, which dotted the riverbank. "There. Sit here a while and catch your breath." Amanda sat with the woman a few moments before adding.

"The view is just as good from this seat, as it is from the bank. Maybe keep back from the edge next time." Amanda smiled.

"Thank you. I will."

"Well, I must be going. Will you be alright?" Amanda asked as she stood up.

"Yes. Thank you again. Goodbye." Amanda walked off with a big smile on her face. Looks like she could prevent something bad from happening. In the right circumstances.

The Plot Thickens

Phil was studying a report back in his Canberra office. The two men exchanging the envelope had been identified. The man seated at the table was Tony Hutchins, an enforcer and associate of a local crime boss, Mario Prestia. The man handing over the envelope was Jack Freeman. He was a petty crim, who was a known associate of a major construction company boss, Marty Jones. The local Victorian police had taken over the case but had agreed to share details with the AFP. Mario Prestia had links to a couple of rogue unions and the police had surmised that the envelope was a payoff in order to keep the unions under control on one or more of Mr Jones' construction sites.

The Victorian police wanted to get a search warrant, but believed the picture, on its own, wouldn't be enough to convince the courts. They wanted more information as to how and when the picture of the two men was taken. Phil was reluctant to pass over that information, just yet. Besides, they probably wouldn't believe him when he told them there was a lady with a phone that could snap photos of the future. The question, Phil kept asking himself was, 'Had the exchange of the envelope taken place yet or not? How far into the future was the photo taken?"

Phil picked up his phone and dialled one of his assistants. "Can you book me a flight to Melbourne tonight? …. Yes. ….. Thanks." He would pay Amanda a visit tomorrow.

The next day, Amanda was in her office when the doorbell rang. Megan was on one of her days off, and Amanda, usually kept the front door locked. People had to ring, and she would come out to greet them.

She opened the door and greeted Phil with a smile. "Back in Melbourne already. How's your surveillance of the couple going?" She asked as she let him in.

"It appears to be an innocent affair. The key date for the submarine project has passed and nothing has happened."

"Nothing suspicious then?" Amanda offered Phil a seat.

"Not that we have been able to find." He settled in the seat and then asked. "I was wondering if you could help me again."

"Oh! What is it this time?" Amanda was not committing to anything just yet.

"The two men exchanging the envelope. We know who they are."

"Some master criminals, I presume." Amanda joked.

"More like petty criminals, but they are linked to some bigger fish. The Victorian police believe it is something worth following up. I have spoken to a Senior Detective, and they have had a stakeout at the restaurant since we altered them of the exchange. But they keep pressuring me for more information. I would like you to go back to the restaurant, with me this time, and video the table again and see what happens." He paused for a moment to let Amanda think over his proposal. "What do you think?"

"It has been several days. I'm not sure my predictions of the future span that far. The events usually happen within a day. The Canberra attack was the only one that occurred the next day. Do you think going back again will show up anything?" Amanda was sceptical.

"As I've said before. The more we test your phone, the more we may get to understand how it works. I'm willing to give it another try." Then Phil had an idea. "Do you wear a watch with a date?"

Amanda glanced at her watch and replied. "No. It doesn't have the date. Why?"

"Well, I suggest we get one for you. I'm hoping, that when you are recording, if you look at your watch through the phone, it might show you the date and time of the event." He smiled.

"Oh. I think I get it." She looked at her watch again. "Will the AFP buy me a new watch?" She asked with a cheeky smile.

"I have a budget. Let's go." Phil stood up, and indicated he was ready to go.

"Right now? Ok. I'll grab my jacket." Amanda headed into her office.

The Twist

After buying a suitable watch for Amanda, they headed for the restaurant. When they arrived, to their surprise, Tony Hutchins was already sitting at the table. Phil asked the waiter if they could sit at a particular table and the waiter agreed. The table, Phil had chosen, was closer to Tony than Amanda's table from the original recording.

Amanda and Phil ordered a coffee each and Amanda started recording Tony with her mobile. Within minutes, Jack Freeman turned up with the envelope. Phil was watching the table and the exchange of the envelope, while Amanda watched through her phone. However, she was seeing a different picture. Tony already had the envelope and was surreptitiously counting the notes. Amanda suddenly remembered to look at her new watch and moved her wrist into the picture. She looked closely, and saw the date was today and the time was about five minutes in the future. She was surprised and withdrew her arm to concentrate on what Tony was doing.

What happened next was a blur. Through her phone, Amanda saw a man appeared in front of Tony, pulled out a gun and shot him twice in the chest, Amanda's mobile snapping the fatal shots. She took a sharp breath at the horror of the scene on her phone. She tentatively touched Phil on the arm to gain his attention.

"What's happened?" He asked. Amanda just showed him her phone and the snapshot of the gunman. Phil looked closely with alarm and asked. "When does this happen?"

Amanda was still in shock but managed to say. "In a couple of minutes. I checked my watch."

Phil turned to survey the front of the restaurant and Tony's table. Nothing had changed. Suddenly, he caught sight of the gunman walking towards Tony. Phil leapt out of his seat and flung himself at the surprised gunman. Tackling him to the ground. The gunman was winded by the fall, giving Phil enough time to subdue him and pin him to the ground. Tony was surprised to see the commotion happening in front of him, but he was cool enough to try to make a quick exit. As he attempted to dash away from his table, his foot hit something and he tripped, falling heavily into another table and chairs. He landed face down on the floor with the envelope still firmly grasped in his hand. Amanda had acted quickly and stuck her foot out, tripping him. Now she flopped down on his back, pinning him to the ground.

"Call the police." She yelled at the dumfounded waiter. Phil looked across and saw Amanda perched on Tony's back with her elbow firmly held down on his neck. "Are you okay?" He half-smiled.

"Yes. Good tackle." She replied with a grin.

Because the police already had the restaurant under surveillance, it was only a matter of minutes before they were on hand to arrest Tony and the gunman. Phil and Amanda dusted themselves off after the police had removed the pair. They resumed their seats in the restaurant and Phil was studying the photo, which was still displayed on Amanda's phone. Somehow, she had managed to keep it secure in her hand during the scuffle.

"Well, that is really interesting. Two different recordings, but ultimately the events were related. See, we are learning more about this amazing phone of yours, every time you use it."

"Any idea who the gunman might be?" Amanda was sipping on a glass of wine. They had decided they needed something stronger than their original order of coffee.

"No. The police will sort it out. They have already picked up Jack Freeman and they now have enough to investigate both Marty Jones and Mario Prestia." He handed the phone back to Amanda. Took a sip of his wine and commented. "We make a pretty good team."

Amanda smiled. "Does that mean I'm in for a pay rise?" They both laughed.

For the moment, Amanda was enjoying her success. However, deep down, she was still concerned about why these visions were happening to her, and what they might reveal in the future.

Under Threat

Confidence

Amanda was at home, reflecting on her recent experiences. *I'm an Emotional Intelligence expert. I know and understand my own feelings. Why do I still doubt myself?'* She looked at her 3-year-old miniature Schnauzer. "What do you think, Sassy? Should I use my phone more often?" Sassy just wagged her tail and continued to look adoringly at her owner. "Well, I know one thing. I shouldn't be scared. Nothing bad has happened to me and I have my business to keep me busy." With her mind now at ease, Amanda got up out of her favourite chair and headed for the kitchen. "Dinner time." Sassy was hot on her heels.

The next day, Amanda was in her office early. She had a lot of work to do. She was working on her new podcast, and she was putting the finishing touches to her paper for a conference in San Francisco. She had been looking forward to this particular conference for over a year, because it was bringing together all the preeminent world experts in EQ. Her draft had been accepted, and she was listed as one of the keynote speakers. It was a real feather in her cap, and she couldn't wait to get there next month.

Her phone interrupted her thoughts. She looked at the caller ID and smiled. "Hi, Phil."

"Amanda, how are things?"

"Good. Business as usual. What's happening?" She sat back in her chair.

"I just wanted to give you an update on our first collaboration."

"Okay."

"The gunman's name was Burt Thomas. He is not talking, and the police still can't work out who he was working for. He is in the remand centre until a court hearing in three months' time." Phil paused.

"What about the guy I tripped?" Amanda took the opportunity to ask a question.

"Tony Hutchins. Well, unfortunately, they couldn't hold him."

"What about the envelope of money?" Amanda was surprised.

"They couldn't prove anything. Nothing wrong with having a wad of cash. The police are still investigating any links between Mario Prestia and Marty Jones."

"Ah well, at least we stopped a murder."

"Yes. Sorry, but your phone didn't really help. No evidence, and of course the police raised more questions than you or I can answer. I'm still deflecting police questions about you and your phone."

"That's why you're paid the big bucks." Amanda smiled.

"Sure." He chuckled. "I'll let you know as soon as I hear any more. I'll be in touch. Bye."

"See you later." Amanda hung up. She was happy that Phil hadn't asked her to assist on another job. She really wanted to concentrate on her podcast and the conference. A reminder suddenly popped up on her phone. She had forgotten about a doctor's appointment she had after work. Her doctor had asked her to come back in a couple of days to check on her head knock. Just as well she had set the reminder for several hours in advance. She made a mental note to leave just a few minutes earlier that afternoon.

Who is That

Amanda left her office a bit later than she had hoped, but she was still on time to make her doctor's appointment. The medical clinic was on her way home. So, she set off along her normal route. As she crossed over the Yarra river, on Queens bridge, Amanda decided, there was no harm in trying out her phone again. She got her phone out to video what was going on around her. Pointing the camera ahead of her, she pressed record on the phone. Everything seemed normal, she snatched a quick glance ahead and it looked like the phone was videoing exactly what she was seeing ahead of her.

A number of people walked past her in both directions and the video showed nothing out of the ordinary. Amanda checked her watch through the phone, and it showed the current date and time. She turned a corner and saw the medical clinic a hundred meters away. On the screen, she suddenly noticed a woman walking, ten or so metres ahead of her. To her surprise, the woman looked a lot like her. She was wearing similar clothes to what Amanda had on. In fact, on having a closer look, Amanda was sure the woman was wearing the same outfit. Plus, there was something very familiar about the woman. *'Is that me?'* She started to wonder. At that moment, Amanda's train of thought was interrupted as a man passed her and appeared on the screen. He seemed to be in a hurry and was heading in the same direction as the woman in front. Amanda didn't recognise the man from the back but felt uneasy and decided to quicken her pace to keep up.

The man was only a couple of metres behind the woman when she reached the medical clinic. As she opened the door, she looked back towards the man and Amanda. Amanda nearly dropped her phone. The video stopped and so did Amanda.

The snapshot on her phone, showed Amanda's startled face looking back at the man. Who was he? The photo only showed his back and there was nothing Amanda recognised about him. She was standing still about ten meters away from the clinic. Feeling a little uneasy she slowly turned and scanned both sides of the street behind her. Nothing. She looked at her phone again and sure enough, it was her, looking back at the man.

Still, a bit unnerved, Amanda, walked to the clinic and opened the door. She hesitated but couldn't stop herself from looking, one more time, back along the road. She breathed a sigh of relief as there was no one there. She continued into the clinic.

"Hello, Ms Staples, you can go straight in." The receptionist ushered her into the doctor's room.

"Hello, Amanda. Have a seat." Jane, Amanda's doctor, closed the door as Amanda eased into a chair beside the doctor's desk.

"You're quiet today. Are you okay?" Jane was a little surprised as Amanda didn't seem to be her usual self. Jane placed a cuff around Amanda's arm and proceeded to take her blood pressure.

"I'm sorry. I'm just a little distracted." Amanda finally replied. The pressure on the cuff released and Jane commented. "Your blood pressures a bit high. Are you sure you're, okay?" Jane removed the cuff and gave Amanda a serious look.

"No. I'm fine. Just a bit rushed getting here." Amanda didn't want to reveal any more.

"Okay. How is your head? Any headaches? What about those ocular migraines?" Jane rattled off a series of questions as she looked closely into Amanda's eyes.

"No headaches and the migraines are happening less and less. I actually feel pretty good." Amanda half-smiled.

"Good. Let's take your blood pressure one more time, just to be sure."

Amanda was soon on her way home. Her blood pressure had come down on the second reading, so Jane was happy to let her go. Amanda occasionally cast an uneasy look over her shoulder, as she made her way home. To her relief, no one was following her.

Sassy was eagerly waiting at the door when she entered. They both settled in for a quiet night in front of the television. Amanda, however, couldn't stop wondering who that man might have been.

A Threat

The next day, Amanda made it into her office without incident. One of the major news outlets had found Amanda's office address and contact details. They had been harassing her to talk to her regarding the Canberra terror attack. Thus, Amanda was even more careful, to make sure her office door was locked, when Megan was not there. When Amanda arrived, she laid out some work on Megan's desk for her, and then settled into her own office. She wanted to review her presentation slides again.

Amanda heard the front door and assumed it was Megan.

"Hi, Megan." After a pause, she became anxious when there was no answer. Amanda eased out of her chair, heart pounding, and slowly headed for the reception area.

"Oh!" She gasped as she found a man standing at the desk. "Can I help you?" She was flustered.

"Sorry, I must be in the wrong place." The man turned to leave. He was middle-aged, thickset and wearing a large overcoat. Amanda didn't recognise him and was about to ask him, who he was looking for. As the man left, he turned and commented. "I wouldn't leave your door unlocked, if I were you."

Amanda thought, *'But, it was locked.'* Amanda was checking the door and was in the process of locking it again when Megan arrived.

"You're as white as a ghost. What happened?" Megan rushed in and guided Amanda into a chair. She ran into the kitchenette and returned with a glass of water. "Here, have a drink."

Amanda did as she was told and looked at Megan. "A man was here a moment ago. I think he threatened me."

"What? Shall I call the police?" Megan was heading for the phone on her reception desk.

"No. No." Amanda stopped her. "I'm not sure what just happened. I'll call my AFP friend and see what he says." Amanda took another sip. "I'm sure the door was locked, but he was standing by your desk. Can you arrange to have the lock changed?"

"Sure, I'll sort it, you sit there as long as you need. You scared me." Megan sat at her desk and watched her as Amanda took another sip of water.

Later in the day, Amanda was feeling better and had finished her work for the day. Megan had just left, and the front door was locked. She grabbed her phone and dialled Phil.

"Hello. This is a bit of a surprise. Have you caught something interesting on your phone?" Phil sounded excited.

"Well, you might say that. I think I'm being followed." Amanda went on to explain her visit to the medical clinic and the snapshot of herself looking back at a man. Then she told Phil about the man in her office and what she thought was a threat.

There was silence on the phone for a few minutes before Phil replied. "So, you didn't recognise the man at all?"

"No."

"Would you like me to come down and watch your back?"

"Do you think this is that serious? I mean, he didn't actually threaten me physically." Amanda was starting to feel a bit uncertain and even a bit silly.

"Well, I was coming to Melbourne in a couple of days, following up on another case. I thought I could come early and see you." That last statement sounded a bit strange, and Amanda wondered about Phil's motives.

"You're better at this stuff than I am. So, if you think you can help, by all means come." Amanda tried to sound lukewarm.

"Settled then. I'll see you tomorrow morning at your place."

"At my place?" Amanda was surprised.

"Yes. Then I can escort you to your office." Phil sounded upbeat.

"Okay." Amanda conceded.

"See you then. Bye." Phil hung up.

Amanda just stared at her phone for a moment. Her mind racing. *'My own escort.'*

The Break In

Amanda didn't sleep that well and got up earlier than usual. She hoped her morning run would clear out the cobwebs. She took Sassy with her. On returning to her apartment, Amanda checked the street just as a precaution and found nothing suspicious. As she went to put her key in the door, she noticed it was slightly ajar. She froze. Was someone inside? She grabbed her phone from its pouch on her arm and turned on the video. She gingerly pushed open the door.

Sassy, rushed in and Amanda dropped her lead. Slowly, Amanda walked in, leaving the door open. The video, showed Sassy running ahead of her and nothing else. Amanda slowly made her way into the kitchen and then into the lounge. There was nothing. Some things looked out of place, but nothing was smashed or thrown on the floor.

Amanda slowly edged her way towards her bedroom, when a hand touched her shoulder. She screamed and spun around nearly tripping over. Phil grabbed her by the waist and stopped her from falling. He steadied her for a moment before releasing his hold.

"What tha? You scared the shit out of me." Amanda was gasping for air.

"Sorry. The door was open, and your dog greeted me at the door. I didn't mean to scare you."

"Well, you sure did. Scared me half to death." Amanda walked back to the lounge room and flopped in her favourite chair.

"I'll be back in a sec. I left the front door open." Phil disappeared for a moment and then reappeared in the kitchen. "Coffee?" He half-smiled.

Amanda was staring at her phone. "Phil. You need to look at this."

Amanda showed Phil her phone. The photo appeared to be taken over Phil's shoulder, looking back towards the front door and it showed the back of a man dashing out the door.

"The phone must have snapped it, as you surprised me." Amanda suggested as she looked closely at the picture. "He was still in the house." Her voice sounded ragged.

Phil used his fingers to zoom in on the man. "Not sure we will be able to recognise him from this photo. Sorry, but there are no facial features showing at all." He handed the phone back to Amanda. "Is there anything missing?" Phil looked around the room. "Anything out of place?"

"I haven't had time to check." Amanda looked at him a little annoyed. "Give me a chance to recover. I'm shocked that someone managed to get in my home."

"Sorry." Phil tried to look sympathetic. "I'll go make that coffee." He left Amanda to her thoughts and proceeded to make them each a coffee. "White and one?" He asked.

"I think I need something a bit stronger. Above the fridge, there is a bottle of Bundy. I'll have a dash in my coffee. Thanks." She nestled back into the chair and Sassy nuzzled her hand. Amanda smiled and gave her dog a pat. "I'm alright. You know, you're not a very good guard dog. Why didn't you bark at that man?" Sassy cocked her ears and just turned her head to one side.

"Here." Phil handed Amanda her coffee. "Maybe it's because the man didn't threaten you. She greeted me at the door with no worries." He surmised.

"Sassy just loves everyone." Amanda said with a half-smile, giving her pet another scratch behind the ear.

Phil sat in the chair opposite Amanda and asked. "Feeling better?"

Amanda sat up and took a sip of her coffee. "Yes. Thanks." She then asked. "Why me? What did he want?"

"Did the man in this latest picture look anything like the man from outside the medical clinic?"

"I don't know. Remember, the snapshots disappear once you exit the picture. I have no way of comparing them. Both photos just show the back of a strange man with no discerning features." Amanda was frustrated. "I'm going to shower and get ready for work." She gulped down the last of her coffee and headed for her bedroom.

Phil picked up her phone and studied the photo.

The Demand

Once Amanda was showered and dressed, she and Phil conducted a room-by-room search. Phil said to look for anything out of place or missing. The search was in vain. Amanda could find nothing out of place. Back in the kitchen, Phil handed Amanda back her phone. "I'm sorry, but I can't use this. The photo won't help. However, what I have done, if you don't mind, is download a special AFP tracking app onto your phone."

"What?" Amanda grabbed her phone. "Why?" Looking at the new app on her home page.

"Well, it's just a precaution. The app keeps a track of where you are and sends it to the AFP control centre. But the main feature is if you open the app. There is a button that sends an alarm signal to the control centre."

Amanda opened the app and in the centre at the bottom of the screen was a red alarm button.

"So, if I press this what happens?" Amanda looked up at Phil.

"An alarm is activated in the AFP control centre. It will have your ID, etc. They will contact the nearest AFP officer to your location and direct them to you as an emergency. Plus, I will get an alert as well, because I'm your 'handler', so to speak." Phil grinned. "The app has other features. You can call the AFP directly anytime 24/7, by using the call button. Someone in the control centre will answer and offer assistance or redirect your call to me."

"My own personal hotline. You think this is really necessary?" Amanda asked a little concerned.

"Well, you have been followed, and had a break-in. I would say, yes."

Nervous and uncertain, Amanda grabbed her things. Said goodbye to Sassy and headed for her office, escorted by Phil.

Shortly after leaving her apartment, Phil asked. "Do you want to try your phone?" As he turned to check behind them.

"No." Amanda was blunt.

"It might show something." Phil was trying his best to convince her to use her phone. But Amanda wouldn't budge.

When they arrived at Amanda's office, she immediately got into her normal work schedule. She wasn't sure if Phil was going to hang around all day or not. Phil felt uncomfortable just standing around. So, he stayed out in the reception area and made a few calls.

"Amanda, is your assistant coming in today?" He eventually asked.

"No, not today." Amanda replied from her office.

Phil poked his head into her office. "Look, I have a couple of things I need to do. Will you be ok, if I head off? I'll be back around lunchtime. We can then grab a bite of lunch." He smiled.

"Sure, I'll be fine." Amanda stood up and followed Phil out to the reception area. Phil gave her a reassuring smile as he waved goodbye. She returned a half-smile and locked the door as he left.

Amanda kept herself busy and the morning flew past. She checked the time, and it was just after 12 noon. Her stomach started to grumble as she thought about lunch. *'Where is Phil?'* She wondered. Just then her phone rang, and she immediately thought it was him. However, when she picked up the phone it didn't display a caller ID.

"Hello, Amanda speaking."

"I've been watching you." A deep male voice spoke from the other end.

"Who is this?" Amanda demanded.

"That's of no concern. Why are you working with the AFP? What's the interest in your phone?"

"I don't have to answer your questions." Amanda was alarmed and angry. "Don't contact me again." She hung up. Her heart was racing.

Immediately, a text message appeared on her phone. "Ditch the AFP guy and we can talk." Once again, the caller ID was not displayed. The message ended with a smiley face, which Amanda thought was bizarre.

Knock. Knock.

She nearly fell out of her chair. Her heart almost skipped a beat. '*I hope that's Phil.*' She thought as she slowly made her way to the reception area. Sure enough, Phil was casually waiting for her to open the door. His smile, immediately turned to a look of concern, as Amanda unlocked and opened the door.

"What happened? You look pale." He asked as he stepped inside.

"I just got a threatening phone call."

"What? From whom?"

Amanda headed back into her office and slumped into her chair. "I don't know. Plus, they sent me a text." She opened the message and handed Phil her phone.

"The smiley face is a bit weird." Phil tried to lighten the mood. "What about the phone call?"

"He didn't say much. He said that he had been watching me. He wanted to know why I was working with the AFP and what was the interest in my phone."

"So, it was a male. Recognise anything?" Phil handed back her phone.

"No. Nothing." She stared at the text message before closing it. "What should I do?" She looked up at Phil.

Phil thought for a moment. "Nothing for now. I will back-off but keep an eye on you from a distance and hope he calls again. I'll get some AFP help to keep you safe."

"What could this be related to?" Amanda was puzzled.

"Well, the obvious thing is the Burt Thomas and Tony Hutchins incident. Burt's in remand, so he's not the one following you, but he can access a phone and organise someone else to harass you. Whereas, Tony, he is out and about. What is troubling, is this person is asking about your phone. Do they know something?"

Amanda just shrugged her shoulders. They both sat in silence, lost in their own thoughts. Eventually, Phil broke the silence. "Are you hungry? I said we would do lunch."

"Well, my stomach was grumbling, but I'm not sure if it's nerves or hunger." She offered a half-smile.

"Come on. Let's have lunch and recap what has happened and think about what to do."

They both stood. Amanda grabbed her handbag, and they headed off.

Taken

Amanda and Phil spent most of the afternoon discussing the events and what steps they should take going forward. Phil kept coming back to waiting for another call and maybe finding out more from the mysterious man. He confirmed that he would do some digging and would definitely make himself less visible, but reassured Amanda that he or someone from the AFP would be keeping a watch over her but from a distance. They returned to Amanda's office, and she quickly check her email, then she decided to lockup and go home.

After seeing Amanda home, Phil headed for the Melbourne AFP central office to start investigating Tony Hutchins and his known associates.

Sassy met Amanda at the door, and they settled in for a quiet night at home. Amanda kept thinking about what she would do if she received another call.

The next morning, while Amanda had breakfast, she wondered if she needed to call Phil before heading to her office. She then dismissed the idea. '*He did say someone would be watching.*' She cleaned up after breakfast, gave Sassy a treat, and set off for work.

As soon as she stepped out the front door, she was on edge. She wasn't really liking the idea of someone watching her, even if it was the AFP. '*What about the other man? Is he watching too?*' It sent shivers down her spine. She quickened her stride, desperate to get to the perceived safety of her office.

Amanda was relieved once she got inside and locked the door. Megan was due in today. She really looked forward to having her company.

The morning dragged. Phil hadn't called and her conference presentation was complete. She and Megan discussed aspects of her new podcast, and potential guests, but it all seemed minor compared to being stalked, threatened and the break-in.

Finally, it was lunchtime. Amanda grabbed her bag and headed for the reception area. "Megan, I'm off to grab some lunch. I won't be long." Megan asked, "Do you want me to come with you?"

"No. I'll be quick." Megan nodded as Amanda left the office.

Once out of the lift, Amanda paused. She had numerous lunch options to choose from. She could head out the front to Collins Street or out the back to Little Collins. She decided that one of her favourite cafés, in Little Collins, was close and would be fine for today. She headed out the back and turned left going the same way as the traffic.

Amanda had gone less than five metres, when she heard car tires squeal and a car door. In fact, it was the side door of a van, opening right next to her. To her horror, a man jumped out, thrust a black cloth bag over her head, and dragged her into the van.

It all happened in a matter of seconds. Amanda was in shock and didn't even think about screaming. As the van sped off, she started kicking and thrashing about. But the man had a firm hold of her. One arm was around her shoulders and the other across her waist. The driver and the man didn't say a word the whole trip, which didn't last long. Amanda guessed it might have been fifteen minutes at most.

It sounded like the van entered an underground carpark and Amanda noticed the lighting changed from underneath the bag. By now she had stopped struggling. Her mind was racing, thinking what was going to happen next.

Interrogation

The van came to a jolting stop and Amanda would have fallen over if it hadn't been for the man's tight grip. The sliding door opened, and Amanda was dragged out of the van. She tried kicking her captor but missed.

"Don't try that again." A deep male voice said close to her ear, making her jump.

She then felt her handbag being pulled off her shoulder. She tried to resist, but it was too late. The man roughly bound her hands together, and then thrust her bag back into her hands.

"Come on." The man commanded and they started walking. Amanda heard a door open and then the man said. "Watch your step." She stubbed her toe on a step. Her curse was muffled by the bag.

They climbed two sets of stairs, before Amanda heard another door open and then she felt carpet under her feet. After a short walk, she heard another door and was pushed through it. She nearly stumbled but managed to stay on her feet. Next, she was marched a short distance and shoved into a chair. She sat motionless, hands bound in her lap, listening for any noises she could recognise. She was nervous as hell.

It seemed like ages before the bag was removed from Amanda's head. It took a moment for her eyes to adjust to the light. She was in an upright chair, in a deluxe hotel room, opposite a middle-aged man. He was also in an upright chair facing her. Her heart jumped as she recognised him as Tony Hutchins.

The man, she assumed, that had nabbed her off the street, stepped around from behind her and handed Tony a phone.

"This is her phone, boss." He then stepped to one side. The phone's screen was off, it was in sleep mode. Tony looked up at Amanda.

"Who are you working for?"

"Who are you? Why am I here?" Amanda was nervous but defiant.

"I'm asking the questions. Who are you working for?"

Amanda thought of staying silent, but then that was pointless. She also wanted answers.

"I'm not working for anyone. I run my own business."

"What about Williams?" Tony queried.

Amanda looked at both men. "He is an acquaintance. I met him in Canberra, while attending a conference." Amanda decided to give them just a bit of information, hoping they would believe her story.

Tony raised an eyebrow and then held up Amanda's phone. "Why were you filming me?"

"I wasn't." Amanda blurted out her answer.

"Don't lie to me." The other man suddenly stepped closer to Amanda and slapped her hard across the face.

"Ouch…" Amanda screamed. She was nearly knocked off her chair. The side of her face stung as she tried to regain her composure.

"Let's try again. Why were you filming me?"

"I.. I was just trying out one of the new features on my new phone. I wasn't filming you on purpose." Amanda looked Tony firmly in the eye.

Tony hesitated for a moment thinking about her answer. "Why did you then trip me at the restaurant?"

"I don't know. The heat of the moment. You don't often see a gun being pointed at someone. I just reacted." Her mind was racing, and words were just spilling out.

"So, I'm supposed to believe, that you and your AFP officer were just having a romantic lunch. For no apparent reason, you just get out your phone and start filming. What, to 'demo' a new feature, whilst trying to conceal the phone as your filming? What do you take me for lady?" Tony had a sly smirk on his face.

Before Amanda could answer, the door to the room burst open with a bang.

"Police! Police! Hands-on your head." Several heavily armed police came charging into the room. One tackled the man standing close to Amanda. The others had their guns trained on Tony, who slowly raised his hands and placed them on his head.

During the confusion and a lot of shouting, Phil Williams had rushed to Amanda's side. He lifted her up out of the chair and moved her away from the action.

Amanda was shaking, but she felt safe in his arms.

"It's over." Phil reassured her.

Reassurance

Later that night, after hours of debriefing with Phil and the police, Amanda and Phil returned to her apartment.

"One thing I still don't understand." Amanda was sitting in her favourite lounge chair. "How did the AFP control room get the alarm from my phone. I didn't press the button."

Phil was opposite her sipping a wine. "That is a bit spooky, isn't it? The control room definitely received the alarm, and your location was relayed immediately to the police and me. Of course, we already knew you were missing. The AFP officer tailing you, saw you being bundled into the van, by Freddie Mason. But then he lost you and we couldn't find the van."

"Remind me. Who is Freddie Mason?" Amanda gave Sassy, her dog, a pat behind the ear as she took another sip of wine.

"Freddie is a known associate of Tony's. Often used as his enforcer. You don't need to worry about either of them. They are both in remand and bail will not be granted for either of them."

"Will I still need an AFP minder?" Amanda half-smiled.

"Let's review it after you return from your conference in San Francisco." Phil finished his wine and stood up. "I had better be going. I have an early flight back to Canberra."

Amanda escorted Phil to her front door. As he was about to turn and leave, she placed her hand on his arm. Their eyes met. "Thank you for everything."

"No worries. Be in touch soon." He smiled, hesitated, but then left her on the doorstep.

Amanda closed the door, leaned back on the wall and breathed a nervous sigh of relief.

Seeing Double

San Francisco

Amanda liked San Francisco, it had a wonderful bay and a nostalgic warm feeling about it. It reminded her of the Sydney harbour to some degree. She looked down over the city, as her plane did a fly over on its final approach to the airport. She had left Melbourne approximately twenty hours earlier. After a three-hour stopover in Sydney, she had struggled through the near fourteen-hour flight. She could never really sleep on long haul flights, even when flying business class. She tended to binge on movies that weren't available on her streaming network at home.

Arriving in the US, and going through the immigration process was tiresome, especially after a long-haul flight. After leaving Sydney at about 2pm on the Monday, Amanda had arrived in San Francisco approximately 9am on the same day, due to passing over the international date line. She was going to try and stay awake for the day to combat jetlag.

The hotel courtesy limo trip to her hotel was uneventful. By the time she had checked in and settled into her room it was after 12. The conference was being held at the Hyatt Regency, in Drumm Street, downtown San Fran and Amanda had decided to stay in the same hotel. The conference officially started on Wednesday and would run through to Friday evening. Tuesday night, there was an introductory cocktail party, every night had some dinner or entertainment available for conference attendees, culminating in a gala banquet on the Friday night.

Amanda had picked a couple of the evening events to attend. She had a list of new people she wanted to meet, plus, catch-up with some of her previous acquaintances. Being a keynote speaker, she was presenting in the morning of the first day. Plus, she was involved in a couple of other plenary sessions, where she would be part of the expert panel.

It was mid-September and Amanda was expecting nice weather for the week. The TV had been on when she entered her room, the volume was turned down. She now flicked the channels looking for a weather channel to check out the forecast. She was in luck. She found a channel where the presenter was just going through the next four day forecast for the bay area. She turned up the volume.

The presenter said the weather would be about average for the next few days, cooling off on Thursday with a chance of a possible morning shower. Friday would be fine and warm. The presenter threw back to the main presenter and Amanda turned the TV off.

Amanda had purchased herself a US SIM card at the airport and had asked the sales attendant to swap her Australian card for the US one.

She also insisted on retaining her Australian number. Once in the hotel, she checked the signal bars and network connection. All looked good. Suddenly, her phone buzzed in her hand as several new text and voice messages came through. After checking the messages and replying to most, she grabbed her laptop and set it up on the small table in the room. She typed in the hotel Wi-Fi code and opened her email. People had been busy while she had been off-line, there were at least 50 emails in her inbox. Before she started wading through them, Amanda ordered some room service for lunch. While she waited for lunch to be delivered, she finished unpacking her case.

The club sandwich was not very inviting. She left most of it as she concentrated on her email. She decided she needed some fresh air and to get something more appetising. A walk down to the famous Pier 39 at Fisherman's Wharf and a chowder would be just perfect. As Amanda walked towards Pier 39, she thought about her phone and her visions. Would she dare use it here in San Fran? Maybe, but not today.

Back at the hotel, Amanda remembered that keynote speakers had been given complementary Regency Club lounge access. As the time was approaching 6pm, she thought a couple of drinks in the lounge would help her relax and maybe sleep better. She changed into a skirt and blouse and preceded to the Club lounge. It was quiet, being a Monday, plus the conference didn't really start till Wednesday.

Amanda grabbed a drink from the bar and found a nice lounge seat with a view out across the bay.

She was reading a text message from Megan back in Melbourne, when she was startled by a woman.

"Hi. I'm Emily. Do you mind if I sit here?" She indicated a seat at right angles to Amanda.

"No. That's fine. Help yourself." Amanda shut down her phone and smiled. "My name's, Amanda. Are you attending the EQ conference?" She hesitated. '*Silly me. Emily, I know that name.*' Her thoughts were interrupted.

"Yes. I'm a keynote speaker like yourself." Emily took a sip from her cocktail.

"Oh. I'm so sorry, Emily. My head was somewhere else. You're Emily Blake, I've read a lot of your material." Amanda was blushing a little as she reached across to shake Emily's hand.

"That's okay. We don't often connect the dots when meeting someone out of context. And by the way. I've read all of your material." She laughed. Amanda joined in.

"It's so nice to meet you." Amanda sat back. "I've been looking forward to this conference and the chance for us to catch up. Compare notes if you like." Amanda emptied her glass.

"Likewise. Can I get you another?" Emily was up out of her seat before Amanda could react.

"Thank you. A gin and tonic with a twist of lime." Amanda smiled as Emily headed for the bar.

A Snap of the Past

After another drink, the two EQ experts found a restaurant and spent a couple of hours over dinner discussing all things Emotional. Amanda also mentioned her new podcast. Perhaps they could work on an episode together. Emily liked that idea. Amanda eventually had to excuse herself as she was finding it hard to keep her eyes open. Emily apologised for keeping her up late and they both agreed to continue their discussions at the cocktail party tomorrow night. Amanda collapsed on her bed and didn't worry about getting undressed. She was knackered.

Staying awake all day seemed to have worked. Amanda woke the next morning with no lingering jetlag. After a quiet morning, Amanda decided the go out for the afternoon. She loved the beach and decided that a nice warm day should not go to waste. She had packed some beachwear, just in case. After getting changed, she headed to the nearest taxi rank.

"Baker Beach, please." She instructed the driver and then settled into her seat. The ride took approximately 30 minutes, straight across town. Amanda asked the driver to drop her off at the North end of the beach on Lincoln Boulevard. She wanted to first go to the Golden Gate viewing point and then she would walk back along the beach. If the water wasn't too cold, she might even consider having a dip. The skies were clear, and the temperature was nudging 78 degrees. Perfect for a walk and swim.

After taking some pictures from the viewing point, of the bridge and coastline, Amanda headed South along the beach and stopped at a spot where most of the people had setup on the beach. Just past the main carpark, but close enough to the restrooms. She sat down on her small towel and removed her sarong to get some tan on her legs. The surf wasn't great with only a few teenagers out hitting the waves. What caught Amanda's attention was some kite surfers. They seemed to be having way more fun, racing along parallel to the beach, jumping the odd wave. She decided, she would take a short video of one of the kite surfers.

Amanda got her phone out and started videoing. To her surprise, looking at the screen, there were no kite surfers, only normal surfers and they looked different. She swung around a little and directed her phone toward the people on the beach nearby. She also moved her wrist into the picture to check the date and time. At first, she couldn't comprehend what she was seeing. The time looked right, but the date was displaying 1991. She refocused on what was on the screen. A family of four sat together on the beach. Parents and what looked like twin daughters. Amanda guessed they were about 9 or 10. The girls were playing in the sand, and everyone seemed to be enjoying themselves. Amanda was about to look away and stop the video, still puzzled by the date, when the two girls stood up and asked their mother something. She responded favourably and the next thing, the girls were running off towards the carpark. Next the video did something really strange. Something Amanda had not noticed before. It seemed to fast forward. When the video resumed normal speed, Amanda saw one of the girls returning to her parents. She was in a state. Crying and trembling. She looked like she screamed at her parents. Her father immediately reacted. He sprang to his feet and raced toward the carpark.

The mother tried to console the girl and they quickly followed the father. Amanda was mesmerised. She stood up, with the phone still filming and followed the mother and daughter. The video went in to fast forward again and Amanda half jogged along to keep up. The mother and daughter moved through the carpark and headed for the restrooms. The father was nowhere to be seen. As the mother and daughter got to the ladies' entrance of the restrooms, the father came barging out, yelling something. Then the video froze.

Amanda lowered her phone and looked at the restrooms. There was no one there. She stepped a little closer and slowly raised her phone and looked at the snapshot on the screen. It was one of total anguish. The father was looking in Amanda's direction and he face said it all. Fear and despair. The mother was reacting to his fear with what looked like a scream. Her hand raised to her mouth. Her other hand was firmly locked around her daughter's wrist. The photo had caught her mid-scream.

The whole episode shook Amanda. She hurriedly collected her things from the beach and got a taxi back to the hotel. On her way back and in her room, she just stared in shock at the image. She dared not close the phone, which would lose the image. Eventually, curiosity got the better of her and she opened her laptop and started searching for anything to do with Baker Beach and 1991.

Immediately, a headline flashed on her screen.

Girl goes missing from favourite San Francisco beach.

She noticed that the search had received multiple hits on the same event. Amanda scrolled through the search results and then clicked on one by a major news channel.

'Police are investigating a possible abduction from a popular ocean beach. A young girl was reported by her parents as missing on the afternoon of 18th September 1991. Police are asking for anyone with information to come forward and assist with their investigation.'

The report continued with a description of the girl and the clothing she was wearing. There were further links to other articles. Amanda flicked through and read as many as she could. Suddenly, she remembered the cocktail party and glance at her watch. "Shit. It's 6 o'clock already." She closed her laptop and glanced at her phone. Oh

No! The screen had gone to sleep. She clicked the home button and to her despair the image was gone. She couldn't think about it now. Grabbing her outfit from the wardrobe, Amanda headed for the bathroom. She would take a quick shower and head out to the cocktail party.

When Amanda arrived, the reception area was packed. One of the catering staff walked by with a tray of drinks and Amanda helped herself to a white wine. Then she surveyed the room, looking for any familiar faces. She soon found one in the sea of faces. It was Roger, one of the conference organisers and he was heading her way.

"Gooood aaye maaate." Roger said with a smile.

"That was terrible, Roger." Amanda returned his smile. "Please don't try and do any more Aussie and I'll not try doing an American accent."

"Oh, but you guy's sound so great." Roger flashed his teethy smile again. Amanda gave him a stern look.

Roger conceded, "Okay, just for tonight. Now, have you met any of your fellow keynote speakers." He took a sip of his mixer.

"I've only just arrived, but yes, I met Emily Blake last night. I'm hoping to catch up again tonight."

"Great, Emily is so much fun. Now, Sergio is here and is busting to meet you. So, follow me." Roger grabbed Amanda's spare hand and dragged her through the crowd.

Sergio was a handsome guy in his late-thirties, he was from Argentina. Amanda was interested in his recent study into Emotional Intelligence in the workplace, especially into the male dominated Argentinian public service.

"Hello, Sergio." Amanda called out over the noise as Roger gained Sergio's attention.

Roger whispered in Amanda's ear. "I'll leave you two. Ciao." He disappeared into the crowd.

"Hello, Amanda Staples. Good to finally meet you in person." Sergio smiled and shook Amanda's hand.

"Likewise. You look a bit younger than you do online." She responded cheekily.

"I'll return the compliment. You are looking amazing." He took her empty glass. "Looks like you need another drink. Come, let's get a refill and find a quieter place to talk." He pushed his way through the crowd heading toward the bar. Sergio ordered her a gin and tonic, at her request, and they found a bench and a couple of stools in a corner.

The evening went by quickly. Sergio was easy to listen to. Later, Emily found them and pulled up another stool. Together they chatted and laughed about all sorts of things. They were only interrupted once for the formal announcement to open the conference. After several hours, the crowd had thinned, and Amanda excused herself. While she wasn't suffering from jetlag, she didn't want to overdo it.

"Tomorrow's a big day. Thanks for this evening. I'll see you both in the morning." Amanda gave them both one last smile and left for her room. She ordered a snack from room service. The cocktail food was fine, but not enough to equate to a meal.

Amanda then settled in front of her laptop and started searching again. She had forgotten about getting a good night's rest.

Researching the Past

Amanda discovered that the parents were Jim and Marjorie Hudson, and they had settled in South Berkeley just after the birth of their identical twin girls. Jim was an IT consultant working for some bank and Marjorie was an executive assistant to a Vice President of an auto parts manufacturer.

They seemed to be an ordinary happy family before the abduction. The media had speculated on what had happened, since the police investigation had gone nowhere. What sort of parents were they? Was there some sort of child abuse happening? Did the girl run away? Why would a mother let her two 10-year old's go to the toilet on their own? The local police eventually referred the abduction to the FBI, and six months after the event, the news stories had ceased.

Amanda did find a follow-up story on the first anniversary of the abduction. Rachel, the twin that had gone missing, was still missing. Jim and Marjorie had separated, and a divorce was pending. In fact, Marjorie had moved back to Denver, Colorado. Taking her daughter with her as she was seeking sole custody. Apparently, Denver was her hometown.

Amanda could not get over the fact that her phone had videoed something from the past. Why? What was the reason? Plus, there was no sound. Previous recordings had had sound. She tried searching for any follow-up police reports, but there was nothing substantial and most articles referred to the ongoing FBI investigation. There she drew a blank. Then she thought of a long shot. 'Maybe Phil at the AFP could find out something?'

She reached for her phone and called Phil's number. She checked the time. Wow, it was after 10:30pm. '*What time is it in Canberra?*' Her thoughts were interrupted by Phil's voice.

"Hi. Amanda. Are you at your conference?"

"Yes. Hi. What time is it there?"

"About 3:30pm. Why the call?"

"You won't believe what happened today." Amanda was excited to explain what had happened.

She quickly described what had happened, with Phil asking the occasional question. At the end he asked. "And you have lost the snapshot?"

"Yes. The screensaver came on and when I went back in, the video was there, but of course it is of the present day. Basically, nothing of the scenes I saw."

"It's odd. You haven't videoed anything in the past before. Perhaps its leading to another video you are going to take in the present and they are linked somehow." Phil surmised.

"Well, maybe. Can you do something for me?"

"Sure."

"The FBI took over the investigation and there is nothing I've been able to find on the internet. Could you do some digging?" She pleaded.

"That's a long shot. How many years ago?"

"Around thirty or so. Sometime in 1991."

"And they never found her? Rachel, I mean."

"No. Nothing reported in the local papers or news channels. But it could have been years later. I just don't know." Amanda sounded a little frustrated.

"Ok. I'll see what I can find. Enjoy your conference. I'll be in touch."

"Thanks." They ended the call.

Some news

Amanda woke the next day feeling tired. She now regretted staying up late. However, after breakfast and meeting up with other conference attendees and chatting about the day ahead, she felt better. She returned to her room, freshened up, grabbed her laptop, and headed for the main conference room. After the official opening, the first plenary session started. It headlined a major keynote speaker, Professor Julia Odette, from South Carolina.

The morning went well, and Amanda's presentation was warmly and loudly received. Afterwards people were queuing to meet her and chat about her presentation. Lunch saw Amanda surrounded by well-wishers and people eager to discuss their own EQ experiences.

Straight after lunch, it was Emily's turn. Her topic was, 'Developing self-attitude and positive perceptions by intrinsic motivation.' Amanda was riveted and felt Emily's emotions as she talked about her own experiences.

"Emotional intelligence allowed me to understand and manage my emotions in order to overcome my grief and self-doubt. By studying and understand the meaning of EQ, it allowed me to develop a self-attitude and positive perceptions to my outlook on life and improved my personal wellbeing. Thank you." That was Emily Blake's finishing comments to her enthralling presentation. A standing ovation followed. Amanda definitely wanted to talk to Emily some more.

Because Amanda's phone had been on silent all day, she decided to head back to her room and check all her messages before dinner. Her phone had been buzzing like crazy.

She immediately noticed several from Phil. She dialled his number straightaway.

"Hi. Did you present today?" Phil asked.

"Yes. It went really well. Lots of future opportunities are coming thick and fast." Amanda was happy with herself.

"You left me a number of messages. I decided to go straight to the source." She grinned.

"Ok. The FBI agent I spoke to was a bit hesitant, as you would expect. He couldn't shed much light on the investigation as it was so long ago. However, I did manage to get him to send me a couple of the reports."

"Great. What do they say?" Amanda was expectant.

"Firstly, in one of the messages I sent you is a photo of the twins. Secondly, the other twin's name is Emily". Amanda immediately thought of Emily Blake. *'Surely not?'*

Phil continued, "The FBI interviewed several suspects. The usual types, child molesters and known paedophiles. Nothing. Their alibis held firm. It's still listed on the books as an open cold case."

"The poor parents, and Emily. She lost a twin sister. Not to mention poor Rachel." Amanda paused to consider the grieve and associated emotions. "I'll go through your messages now. Anything else?"

"The name Rachel Hudson doesn't appear on any register in the San Francisco Bay region. I've done some searching and there is no police record or coroner's report of any young females matching her or her sister's description."

"So, she's not dead?" Amanda queried.

"Not necessarily. But its promising."

"She could have changed her name. Got married. Who knows? Can you keep digging?" Amanda pleaded.

"Sure. I'll let you know as soon as anything comes up. Enjoy your conference. Bye."

"Thanks." Amanda ended the call. She checked her phone and found Phil's message with the photo of the twins. They were sweet and looked about 10 when it was taken. *'Which one is Rachel? What happened to you? Am I meant to help find you?'* Her mind was posing many questions. Then she remembered tonight's dinner party.

"Shit! Look at the time." She rushed to the bathroom and started the shower.

What are the Chances?

The dinner was great. Amanda managed to sit with Emily, and they discussed lots of things. Amanda didn't delve into Emily's past and her 'overcoming her grief'. Instead, they talked more about EQ and the potential for growing their businesses. One thing Amanda did note, Emily mentioned she was from Fort Collins, a small town just North of Denver, in Colorado. Why did that spark some interest?

Day two of the conference, and Amanda had a free morning. The presentations didn't interest her, and she just needed to be back for the afternoon plenary session at 2pm.

After breakfast, Amanda had an idea. *'What if I went out to South Berkeley and poked around? Maybe get the phone out and see what happens.'* It was going to be a warm day, so she dressed in a lite summer outfit. She headed out and grabbed a taxi outside the hotel. The driver took the Oakland Bay Bridge across to Oakland and then on to Berkeley. The taxi driver must have misheard Amanda as he dropped her off in downtown Berkeley. She didn't know her way around and thought it was South Berkeley. After taking a few minutes to orientate herself, Amanda realised she was in the wrong place. So, she entered a shop and approached the shop assistant and asked for directions to South Berkeley.

"Go South along this street, Shattuck Avenue. It's about twenty minutes." The shop assistant walked to the door and pointed the way. Amanda assumed that was South. "Thank you." She said as she walked out the door.

"You have a nice day now." The assistant replied.

It was getting hot. Amanda cursed, as she had forgotten to bring a bottle of water with her. She stopped outside a Cornerstone Craft Beer shop and thought a cold beer would be just fine. It was very quiet inside being only mid-morning. She asked if they served low alcohol beer and was rewarded with a smile and an icy cold beer.

Feeling refreshed, Amanda set off along Shattuck Avenue again. At the intersection of Adeline Street and Shattuck Avenue, she thought, '*this must be South Berkeley by now.*' Adeline Street went off on the diagonal and was a divided road. So, Amanda decided to head that way. She got out her phone and started the video. Everything looked normal. She checked her watch through the phone and the display said it was today, but the time was about an hour ahead. However, what she was seeing through the phone looked the same as she glanced up to look around. There were few people on the sidewalk, and nothing caught Amanda's eye.

A woman in business attire came out of a shop in front of Amanda, turned and walked away from her. Nothing unusual, Amanda kept on walking and videoing. Eventually, Amanda became bored. Nothing was happening and she was about to stop the video. The woman just ahead of her, stopped and turned to enter another shop. As she entered, she looked toward Amanda and the video stopped. Amanda gasped in surprise.

Amanda couldn't believe it. She did a double take, looking at her screen, and then at the shop doorway and back again. The image on her phone was clear. It was Emily Blake. The woman's face and hair were nearly identical to Emily's. Amanda knew it couldn't be Emily, because Emily had a workshop session at the conference that morning. '*Does she have a doppelganger?*' Amanda walked up to the shop still confused. The window was clearly signed 'Rachel Meyers Real Estate'. Amanda took a quick peek through the glass. No one was inside. So, she took a deep breath and pushed through the door into the shop. A warning buzzer sounded, and a young woman came out of a rear office and smiled at Amanda. "Hello. Can I help you?"

Amanda was tongue tied. "I'm… I'm… Is Rachel Meyers in?" She finally got her words out.

"No. I'm sorry. She's out seeing a client. Can I help you?" Amanda's head was in a spin. *'What do I do? I can't just show her my phone to ask if it's Rachel. She would think I'm some sort of stalker or something. I don't want to scare anyone.'*

"Could I have her business card. Maybe I'll give her a call later." Amanda tried to compose herself.

"Sure. Are you looking for a property in the Berkeley area?" The young woman handed over a business card.

"Sort of. Maybe. I'm not sure just yet." Amanda took the card. "Thank you. I'll give her a call." Amanda turned and hurriedly left the shop. She turned and headed back toward downtown Berkeley. She looked at her phone. The photo was still there. She immediately pressed the share icon and selected Phil's email address. As she pressed send, she wondered if it would work. Would the image go as an attachment in the email? The email went, and now the image on her phone had gone. Once again it was just a video of her walking along the street. No image of Rachel.

Amanda went into her Sent items and saw that the email to Phil was there. She opened it hoping for the best, but her heart sank when she saw the attachment was the video. She would call Phil this evening and check to see what he received. Amanda hailed a taxi and headed back to the hotel.

Pay Dirt

In the taxi, on the way back, Amanda did an online search for Rachel Meyers. The obvious hit was her real estate business, but not much else. Amanda tried LinkedIn and found Rachel's profile. She had lots of connections. It looked like she had been in real estate for most of her career. Setting up her own business in 2010, just after the GFC. Nothing was listed about her earlier life, high school, or college.

After lunch, Amanda attended the afternoon sessions but found it really hard to concentrate. All she wanted to do was find out more about Rachel. Amanda excused herself from drinks, at 5:30pm and headed for her room. She checked her phone and there was a message from Phil. 'Call me.'

She called his number straight away.

"Hi Amanda. I got your cryptic email. Who is she?" Amanda nearly dropped her phone.

"You got the snapshot? A woman looking at me?" She held her breath.

"Yep." There was silence. "Amanda, you there?"

"That is Rachel Meyers. She walked in front of me, while I was videoing, and my phone snapped a shot of her. Wait for it. She is the spitting image of Emily Blake, a speaker at the conference." Amanda was so excited. "They may be identical twins. The amazing thing is I've managed to save the resulting snapshot by sending it in an email to you. It's gone from my phone now."

"Wow. That means we will be able to retain the resulting photo. That will really help in our investigations. Great job." Phil was clearly excited.

"What should I do?" Amanda was now unsure of her next steps.

"Well, can you get a recent picture of Emily, so we can actually confirm they are identical."

"Sure. That shouldn't be too hard. People take selfies all the time. I could do that. Then what?

"Well, now we have a surname, I can do some digging into Rachel Meyers and Emily Blake. See what I can find."

"I have already been looking on the Internet. There is not much." Amanda was not feeling confident.

"That's ok. I have access to other resources. Let me see what I can find out. Meanwhile get me a photo of Emily. By the way. Where did you find Rachel?"

"I took a chance and went to South Berkeley. And guess what? It paid off."

"Let's hope so. I'll start digging. Hear from you soon. Okay?"

"Yeah. Thanks again. Bye."

Amanda showered and dressed for the evening. Tonight, she was going to a show. One of the arranged events for the conference. She headed to the Club lounge and had a meal and was ready at 7:30pm in the foyer of the hotel. Many people had gathered, all waiting for their bus to transport them to the organised events. There were several to choose from. Amanda had chosen the cabaret show. She liked the idea of some life music.

Amanda kept searching for Emily. Could she get a selfie with her tonight? She then felt a tap on the shoulder and swung around.

"Hello. Gee, you look great." Emily stood back to admire Amanda's outfit.

"Oh. Thank you. You look pretty swish yourself. Mind if I take a selfie with the two of us." Amanda leapt at the opportunity.

"Of course. Why not?" Emily stepped up closer to Amanda as she grabbed her phone.

"I'll take a couple just in case I muck them up." Amanda positioned the phone, they both smiled, and Amanda took several shots. She and Emily quickly had a look at them. Emily selected one and said, "Can you send me that one. We both look great."

"No problems." Amanda immediately shared the photo and sent it to Emily's phone. "Done. Which of the shows have you chosen tonight?" Amanda changed the topic.

"I'm going to the recital. I like a bit of classical music. How about you?"

"I'm going to the cabaret. Heard it's fabulous." Amanda paused. "How about we meet later for a night cap?"

"Sure. Let's meet in the Club lounge." Emily smiled and headed toward a lady holding a sign up for the recital.

Amanda looked around and found another sign being held aloft for the cabaret.

While Amanda was in the bus, she looked at the photos of her and Emily. She selected one that had Emily more central and messaged it to Phil. The bus stopped at their destination. She would have to wait until after the show to contact Phil.

The Reunion

All through the show, Amanda kept thinking about how she was going to broach the subject of the abduction or that Emily had a twin. Why hadn't they found each other?

Later, Amanda was sitting in the Club lounge. She was talking to Phil. "So, you can confirm they are identical."

"Yes." Phil had printed pictures of the two women and had then side by side in front of him. "I have found some more information about Rachel. She popped up in Foster Care in 1993. After almost three years of being moved from one foster home to another. She finally found a more permanent home. She came out of Foster Care at age 18 and then disappeared. However, I did find a married certificate. It had Rachel Warren marrying a John Meyers in 2009. Apparently, Warren was the surname of the last foster parents she had. She was with them for just over three years and must have decided to take their name."

"Amazing. So, 1993, that is two years after she was abducted. I wonder what happened?" Amanda pondered.

"Yeah, well, Rachel's probably the only one that can tell us that. Now. How are you going to get these two ladies together?" There was a little bit of cheekiness in Phil's voice.

"Damned, if I know." Amanda had drawn a blank. "It does appear like they don't know about each other. Or have they stopped looking. It's a mystery. I'll think about it overnight. Thanks for the great work. I do hope I can get them together. Bye.". Amanda jumped as she looked up and saw Emily standing in front of her. "Hello. Did I startle you?" Emily looked concerned.

"No. I'm sorry. Just been talking to a friend back home." Amanda put her phone away.

"Anything wrong. You look a little worried." Emily sat down next to her.

"No. I'm fine." Amanda paused before turning slightly towards Emily. "Do you mind if I ask you a personal question?"

Emily looked a bit surprised. "I suppose not. What do you want to know?"

"The grief you talked about in your presentation. You didn't really delve too much into why. If you don't mind me asking? What was the cause?"

"That is personal, and I have tried to overcome the pain. In fact, as I mentioned, my studies in EQ have helped me. I still feel the hurt, but I have an inner strength now that allows me to be positive." Emily paused looked down at her hands before continuing. "I lost my sister when I was young. She was more than a sister."

"A twin?" Amanda tried to stop herself.

"What? How do you know that?" Emily appeared agitated.

"I'm sorry. I just had a wild guess. Please continue." Amanda pleaded. Trying to show empathy.

"Yes. She was my twin. It was a long time ago and I don't really want to talk about it anymore."

Amanda pressed on. "How did you lose her?"

"We were only ten." It was obviously still very raw for Emily, and Amanda now started to regret asking. "My memory is patchy. Probably because I was very young and wanted to block it out."

"Was she abducted?" Amanda couldn't stop herself.

Emily looked at Amanda in shock. "How could you have known that? How dare you?" Emily then stood up. "Leave me alone." She turned and hurried away.

"I'm sorry." Amanda blurted out, but it was too late. Emily had gone.

"Shit! Shit! Shit!" Amanda thought she had blown her chances. '*You idiot. Where did my EQ expertise go?*'

After a restless night. Amanda woke the next day and had decided to push ahead. She needed the sisters to meet. So, she had come up with a plan to have Rachel come to the Hyatt Regency Hotel on the pretext of her looking to purchase a property.

Breakfast was over and Amanda was waiting outside the main conference hall for the first session of the day. She had Rachel's business card in her hand. She started dialling the number.

"Hello. Rachel Meyers Real Estate. How may I help you?" The bubbly voice didn't sound like a woman in her forties.

"Hi. I thought I was calling Rachel."

"Oh. You have. Her phone is diverted to the land line. She just came in. Can I ask you to hold and I'll see if she will take your call? May I ask your name?"

"Amanda Staples." Amanda held her breath.

"Hello, Rachel speaking." A rich woman's voice came on the line.

"Hi. I'm Amanda. I called into your office yesterday, but unfortunately, I missed meeting you." Amanda continued to explain. She was here for a conference and wouldn't be able to get back to South Berkeley. She then convinced Rachel that she should come to the Hyatt with a portfolio of properties that Amanda could have a look at. Amanda sweetened the deal, if Rachel came after 5pm, Amanda would shout her a drink in the Club Lounge.

Rachel finally agreed. She said she would build a portfolio of suitable property options for her, based on their discussions.

"Great. I'll see you around 5pm. Come up to the Club Lounge and ask to see me. Bye." Amanda was excited. This could work. Now to get Emily in the Club Lounge at 5pm.

Day 3 and Amanda attended the conference as planned and saw Emily briefly a couple of times. Emily was a bit distant, but not hostile. During the break between afternoon sessions, Amanda summoned up the courage to approach Emily. She found her at the coffee bar getting an expresso.

"Hi Emily. I'm sorry about yesterday. It was rude of me, and I wasn't being very empathetic. Please accept my apology."

"Thank you. After 30 years, you wouldn't think it would be so raw. I thought I had developed enough to cope with talking about it."

"How about we catch up at 5 for a drink." Amanda half-smiled.

They both agreed and Amanda now hoped all would fall into place.

Five o'clock and Amanda was ordering drinks for herself and Emily. They both were standing at the bar with Emily having her back to the entrance. Amanda was constantly looking over her shoulder towards the entrance. Finally, Rachel appeared and she started talking to one of the serving staff. Rachel didn't know what Amanda looked like, so she stood waiting while the staff person went to find Amanda. Amanda gently placed her hand on Emily's arm and said, "I have a surprise for you. Please turn around." Emily hesitated, gave Amanda a curious look and then turned to face the entrance. "What surprise … ?" Emily didn't finish the question.

Rachel and Emily just stared at each other. Slowly, they both took tentative steps towards each other. Amanda could see Rachel's face. Her expression changed from disbelief and shock to one of recognition and joy. Their last steps were hurried. Clumsily, the sisters threw themselves into an embrace. It seemed to last for ages. The sisters quietly sobbing in each other's arms. Amanda started to tear up herself and reached in her bag for a tissue.

Eventually, the sisters parted slightly, not wanting to let each other go.

"I don't believe it. How? Did you know I was here?" Emily had so many questions.

"No. It was a total surprise to me. A lady, Amanda Staples asked me to meet her here."

Emily turned, releasing her hold tentatively of her sister and directed Rachel to the bar.

"This is Amanda." The sisters both smiled.

"I'm sorry I didn't tell you about each other. It was a gamble to try and reunite you, and well, it looks like it paid off."

The three women settled into some seats and spent the evening talking. Amanda listened mostly and the two sisters recalled what happened and how attempts were made on both sides to find each other. The most distressing part to hear was Rachel's account of the abduction and the following abuse for nearly two years at the hands of a sexual predator. Then one day, Rachel's abductor never returned to the house she was being kept prisoner. It took her a couple of days to eventually escape. She ended up in the care of Family Services and then she went into Foster care. Police tried to find her family but drew a blank.

The sisters tried several times to find out how exactly Amanda discovered who they were, but she kept her responses as vague as possible. At the end of a long evening the three women hugged.

"We can't thank you enough. It doesn't really matter how you brought us back together, the fact that we are, is a miracle." Emily smiled as she hugged her sister Rachel.

Cave of Ghosts

Home and Friends

Amanda returned home from San Francisco and was immediately coaxed out to lunch with her two friends, Jenni and Margo. Her friends were eager to hear all about her trip and the reunion of the twins.

"So, the twins didn't try and find each other?" Margo was puzzled.

"Of course, they did. But once Emily and her mother moved to Colorado it became difficult for them. The father, Jim Hudson had a mental breakdown, and the FBI seemed to lose interest." Amanda explained.

"What about Rachel? When she finally escaped, did she try to find her parents?" Jenni asked.

"In the US, back then, Family Services were very state based and there was no coordination between the states. So, Rachel found it hard to find her parents and ended up in Foster care. Remember, she was only ten, when abducted and twelve when she escaped. It would have been hard being alone and so young." Amanda concluded. Her friends nodded in agreement.

"It must have been amazing to see the two sisters reunited." Margo observed.

"Yes. Very emotional."

"Your phone actually videoed something from the past?" Jenni was intrigued.

"It's amazing, something odd is at play here. I still don't know what to think. Is my phone giving me psychic clues? Plus, I can email or send the snapped image. It means I can now save the photo and have proof that something happened." Amanda was excited about the latest revelations.

"Well, now you're back, I think we should celebrate your heroics. Besides, you need some down time. I've planned a weekend away for the three of us." Jenni announced.

"What? When?" Margo was a bit annoyed she hadn't been consulted.

"The Grand Final weekend is coming up, so I've booked two nights in The Grampians. We can do some sightseeing and bush walking. But above all, get out of the city." Jenni smiled at her friends.

"That's just over a week away." Margo pulled out her phone and started searching her calendar. "I'm not sure if I can clear my calendar in time."

"Come on, Margo. It will be fun and I'm sure you'd rather be with us anyway." Jenni gave her a cheeky smile.

"I think it's a great idea." Amanda agreed. "I need some time to relax and collect my thoughts after the recent events. Plus, some news outlets are still trying to get an interview with me. Oh, and Margo, we can even spend some time discussing my next book launch."

"Alright, you have convinced me." Margo put her phone away and they all grabbed their glasses.

"Cheers, to a long weekend away." They collectively raised their glasses.

The next day, Amanda was back in her office. She was finding it hard to get back into her routine after her San Francisco adventure. She had so many names and new contacts to follow-up, plus all the articles she wanted to review. She was dithering about where to start.

Amanda's phone rang, she noticed the caller ID and answered with a smile. "Hello, Phil. How have you been?"

"Good and you?"

"Fine, thanks. What's up?"

"I was just calling to make sure you got home okay, and guess what? The FBI have been hounding me. Apparently, they found out about the reunion of the twins and have reopened Rachel's abduction case." Phil paused.

"Oh! What have they been asking?" Amanda was concerned.

"Well, the obvious things. Why was I enquiring, from Australia, about the case and did I know about the reunion? Also, how I knew you. I kept it pretty vague, but eventually told them that it was a coincidence and that you just happened to meet both the ladies by accident." He paused, then added. "They may try to contact you. I gave them Margo's number as your agent. So, they wouldn't just try and contact you directly."

"Ok, thanks. I should give Margo a heads up." Amanda made a note on her pad.

"Yes. I suggest she keep stalling them and hopefully they will give up. See how she goes." Phil concluded.

"Yes, she's good at that. Thanks. Was there anything else?"

"No. Just let me know when you use your phone again. The recording of a past event is really interesting. I've been wondering if we could use it somehow."

"You know I can't control it." Amanda then added. "I'm going away for a long weekend. I guess, I could try it out on my friends." She half smiled.

"That sounds interesting. Let me know how it goes. Bye." Phil ended the call.

Amanda pondered the idea of videoing her friends to see what would happen. She smiled to herself and thought, *"the weekend could be fun."*

The proposition

The week flew past, and the Grand Final weekend arrived. The three friends drove up together on Friday. They stopped in Ballarat for lunch and arrived in Halls Gap mid-afternoon. They had a look around the town before checking into their two-bedroom cabin at 4pm.

"Gee, this is nice." Amanda commented as she walked through the front door.

"Both bedrooms have ensuites. Amanda, you can have one bedroom and Margo, and I will share the other." Jenni came in dragging a couple of suitcases.

"You sure? I don't mind sharing." Amanda was checking out one of the bedrooms.

"No. Margo and I already agreed. Besides, didn't you say you snore." Jenni chuckled.

"What? I did not. I was joking. Sassy can vouch for me." Amanda glared at Jenni.

Margo came in carrying shopping bags full of supplies for the weekend. "Stop bickering you two. Let's crack open a bottle. I can feel a wine coming on." They all laughed.

It wasn't long before the three friends had settled into the comfy lounge seats with a glass each discussing their plans for the weekend.

"I really want to do the Hollow Mountain walk. I like the idea of scrambling over rocks, plus there are caves to explore." Jenni was excited.

"I did the Pinnacle Lookout walk during my year 9 school camp. I don't mind doing it again. It's an obvious favourite." Margo added.

"If we go North to Hollow Mountain, then we can do the circuit and come back via the MacKenzie Falls. With the recent rains it should be gushing." Amanda sipped her wine.

"Ok. That takes care of one day. What else?" Margo asked.

"How about the Boronia Peak walk? We could do that tomorrow morning and then have the afternoon to relax and sit in a café somewhere." Amanda chuckled.

"Winery is more like it." Commented Margo. "How about an afternoon at Pomonal Estate? They have a café." She emptied her glass. "Refills everyone?"

They all agreed. Once Margo was back in her seat, Amanda decided it was time to suggest an experiment.

"I've been thinking. Would you both mind if I videoed some of our bush walking?"

"What, to get a look into our future?" Jenni was excited.

"No pressure." Amanda could see Margo looking a bit concerned. "After San Francisco, I'm not sure which way it will go. It may be of the past, the future or not snap anything at all." Amanda half smiled at her friends.

"I don't have a problem. Maybe we will see my future partner." Jenni burst out laughing. Her friends couldn't help themselves and joined in.

What is that?

That evening the friends enjoyed a meal in their cabin and each other's company. Catching up on what's been happening in their lives. Margo, feeling a bit nervous, did ask the odd question about previous videos. Amanda tried her best to reassure Margo that there was nothing to be anxious about.

Saturday morning, while having a light breakfast, Jenni asked if they didn't mind switching on the TV. She wanted to catch up on the news. Straight away they were all drawn to the TV as a reporter was standing in the heart of Halls Gap.

"Police have confirmed the 55-year-old man's name is Brian Hillston. They believe he set off, bush walking on his own, on Friday morning and he has not come back to his accommodation here in Halls Gap. The police and SES are searching an area North of the Grampians and we have not yet had it confirmed if they have found his car. We'll keep you up-to-date. The police are expected to talk to the media at approximately 10am. Back to you, Jane."

The TV show switched back to the presenter in the studio. "I wonder where he was walking?" Asked Margo.

"North of the Grampians is a bit vague." Jenni commented.

"I imagine the police don't want a whole lot of people getting in the way of their search." Amanda suggested.

"I hope it's not around the Hollow Mountain walk." Jenni got up to rinse out her breakfast bowl. Margo joined her in the kitchen. "Let's make sure we catch the news tonight and see if they have found him."

After preparing some snacks for their own walk, the friends left their cabin and headed for downtown Halls Gap. Their cabin wasn't far from the centre of Halls Gap and their walk started from the Fyans Creek footbridge, on the East side of the town.

"How long is this expected to take?" Asked Margo as she adjusted her small day pack.

"It's a 6.6km round trip and rated 'medium' or grade 3. The map said about two and a half hours. But that's for the average walker." Jenni gave Margo a cheeky smile. Both Jenni and Amanda exercised regularly. While Margo had a good physique and walked a bit, she was not into vigorous exercise.

"Just don't make it a race, okay. We have all morning." Margo gave Jenni a glare.

They soon crossed the footbridge and headed along a well-marked gravel track. The track wound its way through a Messmate stringybark forest dotted with native pines. After a couple of kilometres, the path became rockier, and they started a steady climb. Jenni was out in front and called over her shoulder. "Amanda, when were you going to start your video?"

Amanda was enjoying the scenery so much she had forgotten about her phone. "Okay." She pulled her phone out of her pocket. "Who wants to be videoed first?"

Margo piped up. "Jenni's up front. She can go first." Margo hoped one video would be enough.

Jenni looked around and said, "Okay. What do I do?"

"Just keep walking as normal. I might start when you not expecting it." Amanda smiled.

Jenni waved and set off again up the rocks. Margo stopped by Amanda's side. "I'll stay back here with you."

Amanda pointed her phone towards Jenni and started walking. She pressed record. Jenni appeared on the screen walking up ahead. Amanda moved her watch into the side of the video. The date and time were the present. After a few minutes Amanda stopped the video. Nothing unusual happened.

"Maybe it will work if I'm not looking over your shoulder." Smiled Margo.

"Ok. Why don't you go ahead and catch up with Jenni?" Amanda suggested.

Margo nodded and set off to catch Jenni. "Hold up, Jenni. You are going too fast."

Jenni stopped for a moment as Margo climbed up after her. Margo had a chance to catch her breath and the two of them set off again. Amanda started the video and was slightly surprised at what she saw. This time there was no one walking ahead of her. "Where have they gone?" She asked herself.

Amanda moved her watch again into the video. This time the date was Thursday, two days ago and the time was 10:22am. As Amanda kept climbing after her friends, Jenni called out. "Seeing anything interesting."

"Not yet." Replied Amanda. She snatched a glance up at Jenni and Margo as they started going around a bend.

When Amanda looked back at her phone, it had stopped. Displayed on the screen was a flash of light blue through the trees around the bend. It looked like a person behind the trees, and it also looked like they were wearing a matching blue baseball cap. There was no sign of her friends.

Amanda called out. "Wait up. I've got something."

Jenni came scrambling back around the bend and down the rocks, followed by a tied looking Margo.

"Is he handsome?" Jenni had a big smile on her face. She was disappointed when Amanda showed her the snapshot.

"There's nothing there."

"Yes, there is. See the blue through the trees." Amanda point at the screen.

"Yeah, but where are we and my future partner?" Jenni complained. Margo had joined them and was also looking at the screen.

"Doesn't it look like a person?" Amanda suggested. "I checked my watch. This happened two days ago. On Thursday." Amanda added as she zoomed in on the blue image.

"I wonder who it is. Why did your phone video someone rounding the bend through the trees?" Margo was scratching her head like the others.

They continued their walk, eventually scrambling up some steep rocks to get to the peak. It provided the friends with a wonderful 360-degree view of the Grampians and the Mt William ranges. "Wow. That is worth the climb." Margo commented a little out of breath.

The friends found a seat each and tucked into their snacks as they took in the amazing vista.

"You can see the Pinnacle Lookout across the valley. It sticks out a little from those cliffs." Jenni pointed across the valley and a bit to the South of Halls Gap.

"I remember it's pretty exposed up there. I hope the weather will be okay tomorrow." Margo took another bite of her muesli bar.

Jenni changed the topic. "Amanda, are you going to try another video on the way down?"

"Sure. See if I can capture that new partner for you." They all had a laugh.

The trek down was uneventful. Amanda recorded another video, but this time it just recorded Jenni and Margo walking ahead. Nothing unusual, which disappointed everyone.

The afternoon was spent at the Pomonal Estate, snacking on a browsing plate and tasting a selection of wines. They got back to their cabin just before 6pm and Jenni switched on the TV, eager to catch the news.

"Leading our bulletin tonight is the search for missing 55-year-old bushwalker, Brian Hillston. Police have issued a statement detailing his description and what they believe he was wearing."

The friends all sat around glued to the TV as the reporter continued.

"Did they just say a light blue baseball cap and blue waterproof jacket?" Margo glanced at Amanda.

"Yep."

"Do you think that's what your phone snapped this morning?" Jenni was excited.

"Maybe. But they say he disappeared North of the Grampians. Boronia Peak is East." Amanda was confused.

"But the video and snapshot were on Thursday. The day before he supposedly went missing. Maybe he did walk to the Boronia Peak." Margo was getting interested.

Of course, there was no use looking at the phone again, as the snapshot had disappeared once Amanda had exited the camera. The news bulletin had also mentioned that Brian's car had been found, but the actual location of the search was still not being broadcast.

"Should we inform the police?" Margo commented after the news presenter moved on to the next subject.

"I've got nothing to show them." Amanda pointed out. "They would have no reason to believe us."

They spent the rest of the evening discussing options, but ultimately came to no decision as to what to do with the information they really didn't have.

Hands of Young People

The friends were up early because they had planned a big day. Margo and Amanda made and packed their food for the day.

Jenni had been glued to the morning news. "He is still missing. We are going around the North of the Grampians today. You never know, we might see the search teams. I hope we can still do the Hollow Mountain walk." She turned the TV off and joined the others in packing their backpacks.

That morning, they set out for the Pinnacle Lookout on foot. The walk started from near the creek that runs through Halls Gap and was rated 'medium to hard' or grade 4. The friends enjoyed the great scenery and the amazing views. Amanda tried her video on the way up and again on the way down. Nothing happened. The up and back trip took them all morning. They arrived back at their cabin around lunch time but decided they would have lunch when they got to the Hollow Mountain carpark. Margo was knackered. "I hope the afternoon is easier."

They drove North and out to the Western Highway and then turned left towards Mt Zero. The dirt road eventually took them to the Hollow Mountain carpark and that's when they were stopped by a SES roadblock.

A SES volunteer walked up to the driver's side and Jenni lowered the window.

"Sorry. This area is restricted. You may have heard; we are searching for a missing bush walker. You can't walk the Hollow Mountain walk until the search is called off."

The friend's worst fears had been realised. Although, Margo was a little relieved. Jenni turned to the others. "What do we do now?"

"Ask the volunteer, if we can still walk to the Gulgurn Manja Shelter." Amanda suggested.

"What's that?" Asked Jenni.

"Just ask." Amanda insisted. Jenni inquired and the volunteer basically didn't see why they couldn't.

"Okay. Park the car here and we can walk to the Shelter. It's not far." Amanda started to undo her seat belt.

Margo was browsing through a travel pamphlet. "Found it. The Gulgurn Manja Shelter is only a short walk. It has some Aboriginal rock paintings."

"Yes, I read about it the other day. There are lots of Aboriginal rock paintings around this part of the Grampians. The ochre paintings include small handprints and animal tracks. Gulgurn Manja apparently means 'hands of young people'." Amanda recalled.

The friends exited the car, grabbed their packs and headed off along a well-worn dirt track. Lunch could wait until they were at the shelter. After a leisurely fifteen-minute walk, they came out through a bushy section on to a wide rock ledge. It sloped up towards some cliffs. They stepped out on to the rocks and headed up the slope, then they saw it, a fenced off area. It was in front of a section of the rock formation that was part of the cliff face. It wasn't a cave as such, but the rocks formed an overhang or shelter. They stopped at the fence and peered through the wire mesh.

"The handprints are amazing." Margo commented.

"The pamphlet said that some these paintings could be over 22,000 years old." Amanda added.

"They are small." Jenni observed as she pulled out her phone to take some pictures. The friends decided to sit on the rocks nearby, to admire the view and finally have their lunch.

"Just imagine, thousands of years ago, people sitting up here looking out over this landscape. It's pretty amazing." Margo stretched her legs and scanned the surrounding plains. She then suggested. "Amanda, are you going to video us today. See if anything happens this time?".

"Sure. I forgot about our experiment." Amanda grabbed her phone. She was facing the rock paintings and started the video. What she saw was the fenced area with the ochre handprints clearly visible on the rocks. But she couldn't see her friends.

Suddenly, the screen flashed brightly, Amanda was partially blinded for a moment. After her eyes readjusted, she looked back at her phone. She noticed that the fence had disappeared. She quickly glanced up from her phone, it was clearly showing something different from what she could see on her phone. When she looked back at her mobile, a figure flashed across the screen obscuring the rock ledge for an instant. When the rock face was visible again, Amanda realised that the small ochre handprints had been replaced with white-painted figures.

"Something just happened." Amanda's voice trembled. Her friends quickly gathered around to have a look.

"What is it?" Asked Jenni.

"It's stopped." Amanda was disappointed. The video had stopped, and the snapshot showed the rock face with the white-painted figures and still no fence. They all did a double take. Looking at the picture and then looking at the rock face with the ochre handprints clearly behind the fence.

"It's completely different. Those figures in the photo are clearly white." Margo observed.

"Also, something flashed across the screen before it stopped. Not sure if it was a person or what?" Amanda commented. "Plus, I didn't get a chance to check my watch. Don't know if this is in the past or future."

"Where is that? I wonder." Jenni was looking more closely at the screen.

"I actually think it's not far from here. Look at the pamphlet." Amanda urged Margo. "I remember reading something about Aboriginal, white-painted figures." Margo pulled the brochure out of her pack.

"Was it the Ngamadjidj Shelter? It's over the other side of Mt Zero, off the Northern Grampians road. They call it the 'Cave of Ghosts'."

"Yes, that's it. Apparently, it's the only Aboriginal rock art, in this area, which used white paint, not ochre." Amanda recalled. The friends looked at the photo and each other rather bemused.

"Shall we go and have a look?" Margo was curious.

"Why not? Maybe, the phone is trying to tell me something. Although, it doesn't make any sense to me yet." Amanda stood up, swung her pack onto her back and indicated to the others she was ready to go.

The friends arrived back at the car and said goodbye to the SES volunteer. Jenni drove them back out the way they had come and turned left at a T-intersection heading towards Northern Grampians road. After turning South along the road, it didn't take long before they found the turn off to Ngamadjidj Shelter. Jenni pulled up in the designated carpark at the start of the walk. They decided to have a quick snack before setting off to the shelter.

Once finished, they headed out along the dirt track. It was easy going and the pamphlet said the walk to the shelter was about three hundred metres.

"I was thinking. The video and the snapshot showed both rock paintings without a fence. I'm pretty sure that means what we were looking at was in the past." Amanda kept thinking about her phone.

"Do you think its related to the snapshot the other day. The flash of blue?" Jenni was leading the group as they started to climb the rocks leading to the shelter.

Cave of Ghosts

"Oh my god!" Jenni was the first to get to the shelter. "There is a man behind the fence."

In a corner, tucked in under the rock ledge, lay a man curled up in a foetal position. He was facing out towards the friends and seemed to be unconscious.

"Hello. Are you alright?" Margo called out to the man as she and Amanda joined Jenni. At first there was no movement, and the friends started to think the worst. Amanda vaguely recognised the man from her snapshot. He was wearing a blue jacket and baseball cap. She also noticed the paintings on the cave walls. They were white and similar to her photo.

"I think he's the man that they have been searching for." Amanda called to him. "Brian, can you hear me?". Jenni was already looking around the fenced area to see if there was a way of getting to him. There was a small gate to one side, but it was locked and chained.

"How did he get in there?" She commented.

"He moved!" Margo grabbed Amanda by the arm.

"Brian, are you alright? People have been searching for you." Amanda tried again.

Slowly, Brian lifted his head and looked out at the friends. "Where am I?" The friends could barely hear him.

"Stay there. We will get help. We cannot get into you through the fence. Don't move. Stay still in case you are injured. Helps not far away." Jenni looked at her phone and then at Amanda. "Do you have any reception on your phone?"

"Not here, but I did back at the carpark. It's about 5 minutes. I'll go back and see if I can make an emergency call."

"Be careful. We'll stay here and keep Brian company." Margo gave Amanda a smile to send her on her way.

Amanda set off scrambling over the rocks and down onto the gravel pathway. She jogged back as quickly as she could. It took her less than five minutes and she sighed in relief when she saw two bars come up on her phone. She dialled 000.

"Where is your emergency?" The operator answered.

"I'm in the northern Grampians."

"What is your emergency? What service do you need, police, fire or ambulance?"

"Ambulance, SES. I think we have found the missing bushwalker, Brian Hillston." Amanda was trying to control her breathing.

"Please stay on the phone. Don't hang up. What's your name?"

"Amanda Staples. We found him at the Ngamadjidj Shelter."

"Okay. I'll try and put you through to the SES controller. Hold on."

Amanda could hear the operation room noises in the background as she waited.

"Hello, Amanda. I'm patching you through to Frank Adams of the SES." The operator came over the phone.

"Hi Amanda. Where are you?" It must have been Frank.

"I'm in the Stapylton Camp Site, near the Ngamadjidj Shelter. We went to see the rock shelter and we think we have found Brian. He is lying under a rock ledge in the cave." Amanda blurted out as much as she could.

"What, behind the fence?" Frank sounded surprised.

"Yes. We are not sure if he is injured. He spoke to us, but he seems groggy."

"We are sending people over now. Also, the 000 operator has called for an ambulance. Stay at the camp site until someone gets there. And thanks." Frank hung up.

The next ten minutes passed so slowly. Amanda was pacing back and forth. Eventually, she heard the sirens. An SES truck was the first to arrive.

"Are you Amanda?" Asked one of the men as he jumped from the truck.

"Yes. My friends stayed behind with Brian at the cave."

"Okay. Jock, grab the stretcher. Pam, grab the first aid kit." People were emerging from the truck, and they all seemed well organised.

"Let's go." The man called out to everyone and Amanda joined them as they set out along the path. More sirens could be heard approaching. Most likely the ambulance.

The man leading the SES team was Shane and he carried some bolt cutters. When they arrived, Brian was still curled up under the ledge. Jenni and Margo were relieved when they saw the rescuers approaching. It was now over half an hour since Amanda went for help.

Shane immediately headed for the small gate at the side of the fence, he made quick work of the chain and lock. Shane stepped aside and Pam went through to Brian first. She started asking him questions about his injuries as Jock and Shane started to setup the stretcher.

It wasn't long before they were joined by more SES crews, police and two paramedics from the ambulance service.

Back at the carpark, after Brian had been driven off in the ambulance, a senior police officer gathered the friends together to take down their details before asking some more questions.

"Did you plan to come to see the shelter today?" He asked.

"No. We really wanted to do the Hollow Mountain walk. But, as you know, the area was blocked off." Amanda kept her eyes down. "We were driving back to Halls Gap and saw the sign for the shelter. So, we came in to have a look."

"Well, it was fortunate you did come in here today. It must have been surprising to see someone behind the fence."

"Yes. Did Brian say how he got there?" Margo asked.

"Brian is an experienced bush walker, but he still decided to go hiking alone. As you saw, Brian was not that coherent, and the details are still patchy. He mentioned that he was doing the Hollow Mountain walk. After looking in the main cave, he slipped and fell into a narrow ravine. He said that was on Friday early afternoon. He was lucky that nothing was broken. However, he was dazed and apparently went in and out of consciousness. When it was dark, someone came and picked him up and carried him for what seemed like several hours. He is not sure if it was Friday or Saturday night. He said he felt like they were flying over the land, not walking. Next thing he knew he was being place under a rock ledge. He blacked out until you arrived."

"Any details about the person that supposedly carried him." Asked Amanda.

"All he saw was flashes of light. Pretty weird. You are free to go." The police officer closed his notebook and said goodbye.

The friends stared blankly at each other. Jenni, finally broke the silence. "Your phone helped find Brian."

Amanda commented. "I wonder what that white flash was. A person or a spirit?"

Margo interrupted their thoughts. "I could do with a stiff drink." They all laughed.

A Hateful Crime

Continuing Migraines

Amanda and her friends had returned home from their eventful weekend. They had discussed many theories about her visions, but in the end, they still remained a mystery.

It was a cold and crisp morning. The sun was just coming up and it was shining brightly into Amanda's eyes, making her squint from the glare. She was out jogging with her new running partner, Depindar, a cyber security IT consultant. They had met several months ago at their local gym and hit it off. Now, they met and ran together most mornings. Depindar was a bit shorter than Amanda, a few years younger, and a good runner. She made Amanda work hard to keep up.

They stopped after their normal 5km run. Amanda was bent over catching her breath. Her eyes were feeling funny. The combination of the cold air and bright sunlight were having an effect on her vision. As she straightened up, she noticed a small blurred zigzag line in her sight, the tell-tale signs of the beginning of an Ocular Migraine. She sighed, closed her eyes, and wiped her hand across her forehead, slightly swaying on her feet.

"Are you ok?" Depindar stepped closer to Amanda and gently took her elbow to steady her. Amanda opened her eyes, "Oh. I've got another Ocular Migraine coming on. It's nothing."

"Again? You sure it's not something serious?" Depindar removed her hand as Amanda steadied herself.

"Oh well, I've told my doctor, and she doesn't seem to be too worried about them. I just need a few minutes, and the fuzzy zigzag lines will go away. I forgot my sunnies this morning, they normally help."

"Well, I'll walk you back to your apartment, just to make sure you make it home safely." Depindar offered her hand again.

"Thanks. I'll be right when I get home and sit down for a bit." The pair set off towards Amanda's apartment, which was just over a block away.

Sassy, Amanda's 3-year-old miniature Schnauzer, was eagerly waiting as Amanda opened the door to her apartment. Depindar said goodbye and Amanda headed inside with Sassy leading the way.

"These migraines are annoying." She said to Sassy as she flopped down in one of her lounge chairs. Sassy nuzzled her hand. "I'm alright. Just need a little shuteye until the fuzzy line goes away."

After about ten minutes, Amanda opened her eyes and her vision had cleared. She checked her watch, got up and headed for the bathroom. Showered and dressed, Amanda grabbed a breakfast bar, said goodbye to Sassy and headed to her office.

Trust

Megan was in the office today, and they were sitting in Amanda's office going over the details for the latest podcast. Amanda was really pleased that Emily Blake had agreed to participate in the podcast.

"Great, I can now send Emily the draft transcript." Amanda finished typing on her laptop.

"Is there anything else?" Megan asked.

"No. It's been a productive morning. Let's head out for lunch." Amanda smiled.

"Ok." Megan grabbed her tablet, her notes and headed back out to the reception area.

Amanda checked her phone. She had it on silent most of the morning, so that she and Megan wouldn't be interrupted. She noticed a few messages and proceeded to open and see what they were about. She saw one from Phil Williams and opened it.

"Hi Amanda. I might have some work for you. If you're interested? Give me a call when you're free. Phil." She read the text and wondered. *"Do I really want another assignment right now?"*

She didn't think about it too long, as Megan pocked her head into her office. "You ready to go?"

"Sure. I was just checking messages." Amanda stood up, grabbed her handbag and followed Megan out of the office.

Later that afternoon, Amanda called Phil, in response to his text message.

"Hi Amanda. Hoped you would call." Phil sounded upbeat.

"Hi Phil. Well, you said you might have some work for me. I'm interested to hear what's on offer."

"Great." Phil continued. "Have you heard of the so-called Bondi Gay-hate murders in Sydney?"

"I have heard about them, and I think there was a TV show that suggested there were 30 or so unsolved deaths."

"Well, there are supposedly many more than the 30 unsolved deaths mentioned in the TV show. Research has suggested that gay-hate crimes actually span a 40-year period starting from the early 1970's. New South Wales (NSW) had a parliamentary committee investigation, which led to a judicial inquiry. Plus, the NSW police have offered a number of rewards for information pertaining to several of the unsolved deaths. A colleague of mine has joined a group of detectives attached to a police task force, which is continuing to investigate some of those unsolved homicides. They have had some successes, but as you can imagine, 30 to 40 year old cold cases are difficult to solve."

"So, where are you going with this? And what do you want me to do?" Amanda was curious, but hesitant.

"Well, my colleague and friend has asked me, if I can help in anyway."

"Why? You are in the Diplomatic Service section of the AFP. It's hardly homicide."

"I know, but I sort of mentioned to him at some point, that I know a psychic who has been very helpful." There was a chilling silence over the phone. Amanda was getting hot under the collar. How dare he tell people about her.

"Amanda? You still there?" Phil asked tentatively.

"So, you blabbed about me over some drinks or something to a mate. What did you say? A Psychic? That I could predict the future, read tea leaves, speak to the dead! Really, Phil, I thought we were going to keep this between us. I trusted you."

"I know. I'm sorry." He paused. "Amanda, you have a gift. I always said you should experiment with your phone and learn what you and it are capable of. We know it can make a difference. Remember Canberra and what about the reunion of the twins. You have already proven its capability. All I'm asking is that you consider helping. Just use your phone and see what happens."

"I don't know. I'm disappointed to say the least." She paused, then added. "Let me cool off and I might think about it."

"Thank you. I really appreciate it. Hope you do have a good think and reconsider. Cheers."

"Bye." Amanda was still annoyed with Phil.

Research

Amanda started to do some research on her own. The literature on hate crimes committed over a 40-year period was extensive. It covered a wealth of surveys, research, books, TV series and investigative articles. They investigated or proposed any number of theories on crimes of bias or prejudice, that target another person because of their sexuality, race, ethnicity, or religion. The NSW inquiry found that there was an epidemic of violence against gays, motivated by ignorance and hate, carried out mostly by gangs of young men.

Amanda put down her tablet and sighed. "This is too much. So many cases. I need a timeline with a summary of cases, but I don't have time for this." She concluded. Sassy was watching her from her basket on the floor. Amanda sipped her wine and thought. *"I wonder if Depindar would help me?"*

Next morning, Amanda raised the topic with Depindar, during their normal run.

"You know I'm a cyber security consultant!" Depindar commented with a wry smile.

"Yes, but you're IT savvy and an expert. Right?"

Depindar conceded. "I do have some software tools that could help search and extract the data." After a slight pause, Depindar added. "Ok. But I'm not promising miracles."

Amanda thought that was rather ironic considering. "Thank you."

"When do you need the info?"

"As soon as possible. I could be heading to Sydney any day."

The friends agreed to meet tomorrow as normal. Amanda headed for her apartment hoping that Depindar would come through and that she'd have the information soon.

The next day, Amanda met up with her two closest friends, Jenni and Margo. Margo had been insisting that they catchup for a coffee. The friends met in one of their usual cafes.

"I'm so glad the elections are over." Margo joined her friends at their table. "The political parties just buy up all the media space. I couldn't get work for any of my clients during the campaign." She continued her rant. "Hopefully, now things can get back to normal." She ended with a sigh.

"You know this happens every federal election. You should take holidays and go overseas or something." Jenni suggested.

"I suppose so." Margo paused and then looked at Amanda. "Amanda, I'm continually being harassed by a journalist. She has been researching you and digging into your San Francisco trip and the miracle around the reuniting of the twins. She is very persistent and thinks there is a major psychic story to tell."

"Thanks, Margo. You're doing a great job." Amanda paused then added. "What's she want?"

"An exclusive tell all interview of course. Nothing less."

"I'm not sure I'm ready for that yet. Plus, I don't like the label of being called a 'psychic'. My Emotional Intelligence customers might question my reputation." Amanda was really worried about the repercussions.

"Well, one day there will be a reckoning and you had better come up with a plausible story."

Jenni was busting to get a word in. Finally, she grabbed her opportunity. "Talking about psychic. Amanda, tell us about this Sydney assignment, that Phil has proposed."

"I haven't got back to Phil yet. I'm still thinking about it."

Margo pricked up her ears. "What? You haven't said anything to me about going to Sydney. Are you going to make my job more difficult by solving some unsolved mystery or something?

"Well, that is actually what Phil wants me to try and do. Apparently, one of his friends is a detective looking into unsolved murders related to the so-called Bondi Hate-crimes."

"What?" Margo nearly fell of her chair. "The media will have a field day. Amanda, please reconsider. Another psychic phantasm, and I'll not be able to protect you. Especially if it's in Sydney."

A waiter arrived with their coffees and the friends fell silent for what felt like ages.

Amanda eventually continued. "I still haven't decided to go yet. I have Depindar doing some research for me. Once I get more information, I'll be in a better position to decide. So, let's leave it at that."

Jenni, immediately change the conversation to try and distract Margo and Amanda.

Sydney

Detective Tony Pirelli was nearing 50 and was an experienced detective. He and Phil Williams had worked together in their early careers and now they considered each other friends. Phil had accidently let it slip, that he had been working with a psychic, after Tony questioned Phil extensively about the failed Canberra terrorist attack.

Investigations had been moving at a snail's pace lately and Tony really wanted a breakthrough. He was looking into a couple of really frustrating cases and if he could just get something, anything that could move the investigation along, it would be very helpful.

Tony had been reading up on Amanda, however nothing in her professional profile hinted to any psychic ability. He was having to rely on Phil's experience and comments as to what she might be capable of. He was also wondering, how he would explain Amanda's role to his superiors, let alone informing the press, if and when Amanda uncovered something.

An email popped into his inbox. It was from Phil.

"Okay." Tony commented after he finished reading the email. In the email, Phil confirmed that Amanda and he would be in Sydney the day after tomorrow and asked for Tony to arrange a briefing for them that morning.

Tony opened his calendar and created a meeting. He invited Phil, Amanda and one of his senior investigators.

The Mystery Man

Amanda had received a briefing pack based on Depindar's research and she decided to take up Phil's offer. After the meeting with Tony and his senior investigator, Amanda and Phil had visited three locations already with no results. Her phone was revealing nothing. Tony started to regret bringing Amanda in on his investigation. He was coping flak from the other detectives. Phil was supporting Amanda as much as possible and telling Tony to be patient.

It was just on dusk. Phil and Amanda had arrived at the next location supplied by Tony. It was a set of public toilets, well known in the early 1990s as a gay-beat. Amanda and Phil left their car and headed towards the toilet block.

Amanda adjusted her jacket and commented. "You know, this all seems a bit sleazy. Stalking around toilet blocks, using a mobile to video who knows what."

"Well, there doesn't seem to be anyone around. Tony, said that there were several bashings and at least one murder, which took place in

- 133 -

and around these toilets." Phil reminded Amanda as they stopped about twenty meters from the toilets.

Amanda just nodded and pulled out her phone. She pointed it at the toilets and started the video. The view through the screen looked the same as it looked today, however, Amanda did notice the surrounding bushes looked smaller. Suddenly, what appeared to be a woman, came staggering out of the men's side of the toilets. She was holding her head. She fell to the ground as two youths came rushing out after her. They proceeded to punch and kick her to the ground. Amanda was horrified but remembered to move her watch into view to see what date it was. She nearly dropped her phone and then the video stopped. The snapshot clearly showed the two youths standing over their victim.

"What did you see?" Phil made Amanda jump.

"It was awful. Here, have a look." Amanda showed the picture to Phil. "I just managed to get a look at my watch. It was October 1992."

Phil was studying the picture. He handed the phone back to Amanda. "Can you message me the image. I'll call Tony and tell him we are coming back to the office."

Amanda sent the image to Phil's phone and then took one last look at the image. She wondered, '*Was this a gay bashing?*'

Later, back at the office, Tony was encouraged that Amanda had finally captured something but frustrated as well. "We know about this one. Tonya Manning was trans. She was thought to be male when she was born, and was raised as such, but often wore women's clothes. Her murder was solved and the two youths you captured in the photo, were found guilty of her murder and have served their time. I must admit, I had doubts about your psychic abilities. But this is pretty weird, the fact that you saw the actual date. I'm impressed. Can you try again, but this time capture an unsolved case." Tony gave Amanda a wry smile.

"I'm sorry Tony. I told you before, I have no control over what I see, or the picture taken." Amanda was disheartened.

Phil tried to be encouraging. "At least, you recorded something. Perhaps, if we go back to the same location, you might record another event."

Tony didn't look that optimistic, but Amanda nodded. "I suppose it's worth another try."

Phil and Amanda were back at the park the next evening. This time they positioned themselves a bit further around and directly in front of the male entrance. Amanda started her video again.

Straight away it showed Tonya exiting the toilets, followed by the same two youths. Amanda endured watching the beating and moved her watch into view. It was still October 1992. The video kept recording as the two youths stood back. Just then a third youth came out of the toilet block. The original two seemed to defer to him, like he was their leader. They were laughing and shouting something at him. He casually walked up to Tonya's hunched up body, lying still on the ground, and delivered a horrific kick to her head. The video stopped clearly showing the third youth in the fatal act.

Amanda gasped in horror at the scene. Phil reached over and took her phone and looked at the image. "So, looks like there is a mystery to be solved."

The next day was spent in the office with Tony and Phil. Who was the third youth? Why hadn't the two convicted youths mentioned that there was someone else involved? Tony had obtained all the police files and court documents relating to Tonya Manning's death.

"Shane Lawrence was the eldest, at eighteen and he received the maximum sentence of 25 years for manslaughter. Jimmy Pratt was seventeen and the trial judge was a bit lenient, sentencing him to 22 years." Tony was summarising the verdicts.

"And where are they now? The murder was over 30 years ago." Phil looked up from one of the many documents he was reading.

"Shane has no fixed address, since his release, nearly ten years ago. He got out early due to good behaviour and has fallen off the grid."

"And Jimmy?" Asked Amanda

"Well, Jimmy has become a reformed character, working in social housing. Helping the homeless and is also an active advocate in the

LGBTIQA+ community." Tony picked up the printed picture of the third youth. "I wonder why they kept silent about this guy?"

Amanda offered her opinion. "He looked like he was the leader. In the video, the other two seemed to defer to him."

"It's a pity that I can't see the video. I'm not sure we will ever discover whom this person is." Tony said as he continued to gaze at the picture.

"We can use the picture and run it through our databases." Phil suggested.

"What about Jimmy Pratt?" Amanda asked. "You could show him the picture and see if he will spill the beans."

"Highly unlikely. Remember he did nearly 20 years in prison for this guy." Tony handed Phil the photo.

Phil commented. "You never know. You said he was a reformed character. The photo might tug on his conscience."

"Alright, I'll see what I can organise." Tony was sceptical.

Their thoughts were interrupted when a police officer knocked and then entered the room. "Sir. Several media outlets have heard there has been a breakthrough in a case. They want to know if you are going to call a media conference or release a statement."

Tony looked annoyed. "How the hell did they find out about this? I was hoping to keep a lid on this for a while yet."

Phil commented. "Sounds like the walls around here have ears. We should be more careful as we proceed."

Tony turned to the officer. "Tell them a statement will be release when I'm ready. These are delicate investigations, and I will not be rushed."

"Yes, sir." The officer wasn't happy with the response. Now he had to go and deliver the bad news to the waiting media.

Phil waited for the door to close behind the officer. "We need to speak to Jimmy Pratt asap."

"Yes. I'll see what I can arrange. Meanwhile, Phil, if you could get some of your contacts to run the photo image through their databases. It could save us a lot of extra digging."

"Sure." Phil acknowledged.

"What do you want me to do next?" Amanda asked. "Should I go back and video the scene again. It might reveal something else."

"You're the psychic. I'll leave that up to you." Tony said as he left the office. Amanda cringed again at the term 'psychic'.

"You should remind your friend, that I'm not a psychic." Amanda suggested to Phil as she grabbed her things and left the office.

New Evidence

Amanda and Phil had returned to the toilet block at dusk to try and collect more evidence. This time Amanda stood in a different location from the previous times to see what would happen. To Phil's and her surprised the video started after the fatal kick had been delivered. Shane and Jimmy were looking on in horror. As with previous videos of the past, there was no sound. Amanda just saw the looks on their faces and they started yelling at the third man. He swung around at them and yelled something in return. Maybe a threat because they both stopped yelling. The third man then started running and the other two reluctantly followed.

"Come on. We need to follow them." She instructed Phil.

The three men ran and jumped into a car. Phil was trying to keep up with Amanda and watch over her shoulder. As the car started, Amanda yelled over her shoulder. "Quick get your car."

Luckily, Phil's car was only two cars away. He scrambled into the driver's seat and gunned the engine. Amanda was standing on the kerb, waving her arm for him to hurry. Phil screeched to a holt, and she jumped in. She yelled in his ear. "Quick the video is gone into fast forward. Drive straight and then turn at the first right. We cannot lose them."

Phil was driving blind. There was nothing in front of him. Amanda yelled instructions as Phil did his best to follow an imaginary car. After what seemed ages, but was really only about ten minutes, Amanda told him to stop. "They have stopped, there." She pointed. "Oh no. The video has stopped".

Amanda was just staring at the screen. Phil parked the car and stopped the engine. "Let's have a look." He asked.

Amanda showed him the image. "That's our third man." He explained.

"Yes. He is entering that house. How is this going to help us?" Amanda sounded despondent.

"Easy. We find out who lived here back in October 1992. Then we've got our man." He smiled at Amanda.

Amanda had taken note of the car registration number and Phil added it to his notepad along with the address the third man had entered. He turned to Amanda. "Well, that was fast and furious. I hope this gives us the breakthrough Tony is looking for."

Phil started the car, and they headed back to the police headquarters.

Tony was waiting excitedly in his office as they returned. Phil had called ahead to inform Tony they had a breakthrough.

"Well, come on. Don't keep me in suspense anymore. What have you got?" He ushered them into his office and closed the door.

"You wouldn't believe it. Amanda and her phone led us to the mystery man's probable address at the time of the attack. I'm continually amazed at what they can do." Phil smiled at Amanda.

Phil took out his notepad, opened it at the page with the details and passed it over to Tony.

"We've got the car rego and the address." Amanda added.

"Not sure how we are going to use this. But we can try." Tony opened a file on his desk. Shuffled through some papers and found what he was looking for. "The rego matches." He showed Phil and Amanda the rego of the car, Shane and Jimmy were in when they were stopped the next morning.

"Great. That at least provides a link between the two arrested and this mystery third person. How long before you get detail of the people living at the address." Phil was eager for a result.

Just then Phil's mobile rang. He excused himself as he answered the call.

"Hi. What have you got?" He paused listening to the caller.

"Okay. Thanks. Keep looking, something might pop up. Bye." Phil returned to his seat.

"They haven't found a match to the photo. Looks like our suspect had a clean slate in his youth. Also, because social media wasn't around back then, there is nothing on the web." Phil expressed his disappointment.

While Phil was taking his call, Tony had entered the address into his computer, searching for the owners.

"Good news, the current owners have been in the house since the mid-1980s, and they are still there." Tony looked up from his computer.

"How are you going to approach them?" Amanda was curious.

"Who are they?" Phil asked.

"Noel and Betty Salmon. They are now in their late 70s." Tony reached for his phone. "I'll get some of my people to look into their background a bit more and see how we can devise a reason to go calling."

A Media Crush

Nothing had turned up against the Salmons. They seemed to be an ordinary couple with two children, a girl and boy, both now adults in their 50s. None of them had turned up in any police files.

"Maybe it's the wrong address. The mystery man could have been visiting or gone through the property as a shortcut, or who knows what." Tony was frustrated.

"Can't we get to meet the Salmons? Any excuse to get inside. Amanda could use her skills to uncover something." Phil was also frustrated that they seemed to have hit a roadblock.

"You still have Jimmy Pratt. Can you at least confront him with the photo and see what happens?" Amanda reminded them.

"Okay. We know Jimmy goes to a halfway house in the afternoons. Let's head down there today." Tony agreed.

Jimmy reluctantly agreed to talk to them only once Tony explained they were investigating a number of hate-crimes and his knowledge of the scene at the time could be of assistance. They sat in a small office as Tony asked questions. Most of the time Jimmy remain vague, then Tony said. "If you don't mind, I would like you to have a look at this photo." Jimmy took in a sharp breath as soon as he saw the face. "What tha! Where did you get that?" Jimmy backed up in his seat, displaying signs of discomfort.

"Never mind." Tony sat forward. "You obviously recognise him. Who is he?"

There was a long silence. Amanda could see Jimmy battling with his inner thoughts and feelings.

Phil broke the silence. "Does the name Salmon mean anything to you."

Jimmy flash Phil a glance. "I cannot help you. Leave me alone." Jimmy yelled as he hastily left the office.

"Well, I would say that's a yes. Wouldn't you?" Tony snapped up the photo. "We definitely need to speak with the Salmons."

As Tony, Phil and Amanda left the building, they were confronted by a group of reporters accompanied by camera crews. The gathered media rushed to question Tony.

"Detective Pirelli, can you give us a statement on your latest inquiries?" One of the reporters yelled out over the noise. Another yelled. "Why are you questioning Jimmy Pratt?"

Tony was puzzled as to how they knew they were there. He motioned to Phil and Amanda to stay back behind him as he moved to address the group. He raised his hand to quieten the crowd.

"As you know, the task force has been following a number of inquiries into the so called 'hate-crimes'. We are checking back over old cases to see if any recent information has any bearing. Today we were just covering some old ground. I have nothing new to report at this stage."

A reporter, by the name of Maxine Truman, pushed her way forward through the crowd and asked. "Is it true you are using a psychic in your investigations?" Amanda tried not to react.

"No comment. Thankyou." Tony was trying to close down the gathering. He turned to leave. Maxine pushed ahead with another question. "What skills does the psychic have and what have they revealed?"

"As I said. No comment. I will call a press conference soon, when I have concrete information to share. That will be all. Good day." Tony walked off and signalled for Phil and Amanda to follow. They had to push their way through the gathered media pack as more questions were yelled at them.

"Detective, who are these two people?"

"Is one of them the psychic?"

"Madam, are you the psychic?"

Cameras clicked and people jostled for position to question them. Amanda tried to shield her face as they moved towards Tony's car. Once in the car, Tony drove his car carefully through the media crush and finally out into the street and on their way.

"Shit! How did they know we were here?" Tony was not happy.

"You really need to find the leak in your team." Commented Phil.

"Not helping." Tony replied.

"I knew I shouldn't have got involved. What's this going to do to my business? I think I'll return to Melbourne as soon as possible." Amanda was considering her position.

"Amanda, please." Phill turned to face her. "You helped uncover a key piece of information. Don't you want to see it through? Don't you want to know who the mystery man is?"

Amanda's mind was racing over the implications of her involvement. She shrugged her shoulders, turned away and looked out the window in silence, as they headed back to Tony's office.

Revelation

They settled into Tony's office. Tony was still angry about the confrontation with the media. "That Maxine Truman, she's relentless. It's not going to be easy to get her off this case." He commented to Phil. Tony's phone rang interrupting Phil's response.

"Hi. What have you got?" Tony listened to the caller. "Ok. We will try that. How soon can you arrange it? .... Oh! Tomorrow. That's great. Thanks. Bye."

"News?" Phil asked.

"Yes. The Salmon couple get meals-on-wheels once a week. We've got permission to send someone along as part of a welfare visit." Tony looked at Amanda. "Do you feel up to visiting this couple and seeing what you can find out?"

Amanda was jolted out of her thoughts. "What, me?"

"Yes. We can't send in anyone officially. No police. But you can be sent in as a community volunteer."

"I don't know. I just can't go in there and start asking questions about hate-crimes. Or flash them the photo and ask if this man lived there. How will me visiting give us anything?" Amanda was very sceptical.

"I don't have any answers for you, Amanda, but it's an opportunity we cannot miss. Just be observant, maybe ask them subtly about their family."

"I'm not using my phone, whatever happens." Amanda was adamant.

"Sure." Tony looked at Phil. "I will organise the details for tomorrow. Go back to your hotel and stay low. I'll get someone to take you out the back way. Let's avoid any more press."

Phil and Amanda gathered their things and left.

The next day Amanda was driven to the Salmon's house by a social worker. During their trip the social worker filled Amanda in on the routine and gave her some background about the Salmons. Amanda was going to deliver the meals on her own. The social worker said that the Salmons were very friendly and loved a chat. They usually invited the person delivering the meals in for a cuppa and chat. Amanda agreed that she would go inside to see what she could find.

"Hello. You're new." Betty Salmon answered the door.

"Hello. Well, I'm just filling in for today." Amanda replied.

"Well, come in and I'll put the kettle on. We like to see new faces." Betty left Amanda to let herself in as she wandered off into the house.

"Noel. Meals on wheels are here." Betty called out.

Noel came out of a room as Amanda tentatively followed Betty into the house.

"Hello, I'm Amanda."

"Welcome. Let me take those." Noel took the basket and a pot that Amanda was carrying. "Follow me." Noel turned and headed further into the house.

Once in the Kitchen, Noel unpacked the basket and put most things in the fridge. Betty was busying herself getting cups, plates and what looked like a cake tin. She laid everything out on the kitchen table and directed Amanda to sit on one of the chairs.

"Sorry. I forgot to ask your name." Betty asked as the kettle started to whistle.

"I'm Amanda. Thankyou. I wasn't expecting this." Amanda was quite surprised at the Salmon's warm welcome.

Amanda and the couple engaged in idle chit chat over a cuppa. Amanda kept trying to look for an angle to ask them about their family. It wasn't easy because she didn't want them to feel like she was prying. Eventually, it came time for Amanda to leave. This time Betty led them through the main lounge. Amanda noticed a lot of what looked like family photos on the wall and on a sideboard. She jumped at the opportunity. "What lovely photos. Are these your family?" She asked as she stepped towards the sideboard for a better look.

"Yes. Mostly." Betty replied as she followed Amanda. "This is our daughter Jenny and our son Edward." She pointed out their two children. The picture seemed relatively recent as Amanda thought they looked middle aged.

Noel joined them and commented. "Of course, you may recognise our son. He was elected to the senate in the election, just passed." Noel sounded very proud. Amanda didn't recognise the man in the photo. Besides there are many people elected to the senate. However, she feigned recognition. "Oh. Yes. Now you mention it."

Betty added. "He ran for the Christian Democratic party. He took the last seat from the One Nation candidate. He has very strong Christian beliefs." Noel wandered over to the photos on the wall and pointed to a formal family group photo.

"This was taken when Betty and I became elders in our local church." He commented.

Amanda had to stop herself from gasping. There in the photo was a young man she recognised. To make it less obvious of her interest in the man, Amanda pointed to their daughter. "Is that your daughter Jenny?"

"Yes, and that's Edward. Jenny was 20 and Edward 18 back then." Noel replied.

"It's a lovely family photo." Amanda smiled and waited to be shown out. Betty got the hint and headed for the front door.

"It's been lovely to meet you. Hope you come around some other time." Betty opened the door allowing Amanda to pass through.

"It was lovely to meet you also. Have a nice day." Amanda couldn't wait to get in her car. However, she took her time and tried to look casual as she walked out the gate.

Once in her car, she checked to see Noel and Betty had closed the door, and immediately dialled Phil's number.

"Hello." Phil answered.

"I've uncovered the mystery man." Amanda had a big smile on her face.

"Come on. Don't keep me in suspense."

"Newly elected Senator Edward Salmon." The phone went silent.

"Phil? Are you still there?"

"Yes. My mind is racing. Come straight back to Tony's office and let's regroup. See you soon."

"Okay. Bye." Amanda was a little surprised by Phil's reaction.

Back in Tony's office, Amanda outlined her visit with the Salmons. She confirmed that the young man in the family photo she saw matched the mystery man.

Tony was scratching his head. "I'm not sure what I can do with this. It's great that we know who the mystery man is. But we have no tangible evidence that would allow me to open an investigation into Senator Salmon."

"I suggest you try Jimmy Pratt again. Or track down Shane Lawrence." Amanda then turned to Phil. "My work here is done. I must get back home. I have a business to run." She stood up and gathered her things.

"Amanda, surely you want to see this through. We are very close to getting a resolution." Phil was pleading.

"I'm sure Tony can manage without me. I gave you the clues and that's that. I don't like all this media attention. I have my business to think about. Sorry." Amanda walked out of the office.

Tony reminded Phil. "You'd better take her out the back way. Reporters are bound to be hanging around."

"Okay. I'll be back shortly." Phil hurried after Amanda.

Phil caught up to Amanda and directed her out the back. This time Maxine Truman and her crew were waiting.

"Can you comment on the Tonya Manning case? Have you uncovered new information?" Maxine just started firing questions as Phil and Amanda tried to exit the building.

"No comment." Phil ushered Amanda down the street towards his car.

"Madam, are you a clairvoyant? In what capacity are you helping the police?" Maxine then changed her attack to Phil. "Why is the AFP involved in this case?"

Phil repeated his answer. "No comment." As they finally made it to his car. The camera man snapped off a couple of more photos of Amanda as she sat waiting for Phil to drive off.

The car pulled away leaving Maxine and her crew in their wake.

"Do you think they know?" Amanda asked Phil.

"If there is a leak in Tony's office, they might. Let's hope they haven't found out about the Salmons. Tony's going to have to work hard to keep a lid on this."

"I just hope this isn't going to affect my business." Amanda was worried.

Past Sins

Amanda was back in her apartment; she had tuned in to the evening news.

"Tonight, we can report that a NSW police task force, investigating the so-called Bondi Gay-hate crimes, have engaged a psychic to assist them in a case. The case was thought to be closed, and two men had been convicted of murdering Tonya Manning, in October 1992. However, new information has led police to belief there was another person involved in the murder. The investigation is ongoing and as more details come to light, we will bring you that story." The news presenter then moved onto the next item.

Amanda had a sick feeling in her stomach. She had been getting calls from different media outlets trying to confirm her involvement in the Tonya Manning investigation. Margo, her publicist, had been trying hard to shield her from the frenzy. Amanda's phone rang and she saw Phil's number displayed.

She answered. "Hi. What's the latest?"

"Tony has had a breakthrough and has located Shane Lawrence. He plans to interview him tomorrow." Phil sounded upbeat.

"That's good. What about Jimmy Pratt?" Amanda's stomach was starting to settle.

"Still a work in progress. Tony thinks he can wear him down. Let's see what happens after Tony talks to Shane."

"The news is now reporting a psychic is involved. I don't suppose the heat is going to die down soon."

"Sorry, Amanda. I didn't think you would get this sort of attention. If it gets out of hand, I could contact someone in the Victorian police and see if they can provide some protection."

"The attention is one thing; my business reputation is another." Amanda then reflected. "I suppose the result of my visions were going to be noticed at some point. I'll have to get used to it."

"Sounds positive. I'll keep you up to date with developments. Bye."

Amanda didn't have time to think about Phil's news for long. Her phone rang again.

"Hi Margo." Amanda answered. "I suppose you saw the news?"

"Amanda darling. How are you holding up?"

"I think I've come to the realization that this is inevitable. But I'm not sure how my business clients will react."

"Amanda, they love you. I don't think that will change." Margo paused. "I actually rang to warn you. Maxine Truman, once she gets a sniff, she is like a terrier. I think she is ready to go public and name you. Plus, I think she has a scoop as to the identity of the mystery man."

There was a long pause as the information sank in. "Amanda?" Margo eventually broke the silence.

"Yes. I heard you. We can only wait and see now. Tomorrow is going to be a big day." Amanda suggested.

"Hang in there, girl. I'll call tomorrow. Bye." Margo signed off.

Amanda didn't sleep that well and woke early. She met Depindar for their morning run and once she returned home, she turned the TV on to catch the news.

"Breaking news this morning. Amanda Staples has been identified as the psychic used in the Tonya Manning case. Ms Staples is a renown Emotional Intelligence expert here in Melbourne. The clairvoyant has allegedly uncovered new evidence in the Tonya Manning murder. This has led NSW police to interview the two men convicted on the murder over 30 years ago. Allegedly, a mystery third man was involved. We can now reveal a shocking revelation that police belief the mystery man is none other than newly elected Senator Edward Salmon. We are still waiting to hear a response to this allegation from the Senator. However, we do know that Senator Edward Salmon has taken leave from the Senate as a criminal investigation has now been initiated into his involvement in one or more of the Bondi Gay-hate crimes. We will bring more updates on this story as soon as they come to hand." The news bulletin went to an ad break.

Phil's name came up on Amanda's phone. "Hi. Sorry, the cat's out of the bag."

Hounded & Harassed

The Fall Out

Amanda was just leaving her apartment to go to her office when she got a surprise call from Megan.

"Amanda, I'm at the office and there are people from the media everywhere. I thought I should warn you." Megan sounded flustered.

"Are you ok?"

"Yes. I've managed to keep them out of the office so far."

"How come you are at the office this early?" Amanda was puzzled.

"With all the news and everything, I thought I would come in early and see what I could do to help."

"Thanks, that's nice of you." Amanda had gone back into her apartment. "I was going to come in, but on second thoughts, I might stay home. Maybe the media will lose interest after a while. Let me know if they leave." Amanda had a quick think, then added. "Oh, there are a couple of files on my laptop in the office. They are in the folder for my new book. Could you email them to me. I'll work on them from my tablet. Otherwise, don't say anything to the media. Let me know when you leave the office. Thanks again."

"Sure. I'll keep you up to date. Bye."

Amanda didn't have a moment to collect her thought before her phone rang again.

"Hi Margo. The media are camped outside my office."

"I figured as much. So, are you at home?" Margo sounded breathless and there was a lot of background noise.

"Yes. Megan is in the office and warned me. Where are you?" Amanda was curious.

"Oh, I'm at a media launch, but that doesn't matter. Maxine Truman has contacted me and wants to setup a one-on-one exclusive interview with you. She is willing to pay." Margo paused to let that sink in.

"Margo, I'm not sure. I mean what do I tell her. I don't consider myself a psychic." Amanda was reluctant.

"That's good. I was going to advise against it. I think it would be a trap. Once Maxine sits you down, I think she will go hard and try to discredit you. Most people don't believe in psychics, and many believe they are frauds. The problem is, if you don't tell your own story, then the media will make it up. It's going to get messy either way."

"Thanks for your advice. I think I'll ride it out. Lay low and hope the attention will die down. I mean surely, this is not a big story."

"Don't underestimate the ramifications of your discovery. Senator Salmon is denying everything, and you've said yourself, that the police are going to find it hard to use your information against him. But this is still a big scandal. So, be prepared to feel some heat. I'll keep deflecting and delaying as much as I can."

"Thanks Margo. I really appreciate your help." Amanda was feeling reassured that Margo was in her element.

"That's what friends are for. Talk soon. Bye." Margo was gone.

Amanda checked her emails and was surprised at the number. She found the email from Megan with her files but was distracted by the numerous emails from strangers wanting her to help them. Many of them wanted her to do a psychic reading for them.

Amanda closed her email and wondered what would happen next.

Pressure Mounts

After a couple of cups of coffee and reviewing the files, Megan had sent her, Amanda circled back to the growing list of emails. She was surprised at how many people were desperate to either, commune with a dead relative or find out what their future holds. It was just on noon, so Amanda turned on the TV to catch the midday news.

It wasn't long before the news presenter moved on to the unfolding story involving Senator Salmon and the Bondi Gay-hate crimes.

"Senator Edward Salmon, in a media interview this morning, has again denied all allegations against him. He attacked the NSW police and their use of a fake psychic in their investigations. The Senator has also issued a challenge to the so called 'psychic' to come forward, so he can confront them and prove that they are a fraud. The NSW police have responded by issuing another statement. They say that the use of a psychic is not unusual in cold cases and that their investigations are ongoing. The psychic being named by some media outlets is Amanda Staples. At this stage, she has not issued any statements. More news to follow after this short break."

Amanda turned the TV off. Her mind was racing. '*Should I respond? How can I defend myself?*' She had no answers. Her thoughts were interrupted again by her phone.

She didn't recognise the number and hesitated before giving into curiosity and answering.

"Hello?"

"Amanda Staples. This is Maxine Truman. I'm outside your apartment. Can we meet and talk. I have a proposition for you." There was deadly silence on the phone. Amanda was tempted to hang up.

"Okay. Let me grab my things and I'll be out in a moment." Amanda was being drawn to the flame like a moth.

"Thanks." Maxine ended the call.

Once outside, Amanda and Maxine exchanged an awkward greeting before Maxine suggested they go for a quite coffee. They walked in silence as Amanda led the way to a local café. Both eyeing each other, trying to get a reading on the others intent.

They ordered and paid for their coffees then found a table in a back corner. Maxine kicked off the discussions with a statement. "Today's chat is off the record. Let's keep it informal. I'm interested in your background and what are your motives."

Amanda was feeling uneasy. Maxine was a confident and imposing woman. She needed to be careful.

"Well, I could ask you the same. What are your motives?" Her strategy would be to counter questions with questions of her own.

Maxine smiled. "We're not going to get very far, if we continue to dance around each other." She paused then added. "I'm an investigative reporter and feel I have a duty to bring newsworthy stories to the public. I'm ambitious and have a reputation to maintain. Your involvement in the Sydney Gay-hate investigations has sparked my interest. Plus, there is a potential scandal involving a federal Senator. So, what are you willing to tell me?"

Amanda took a moment to collect her thoughts. "Firstly, I don't consider myself a psychic. So, let's not go into aspects of the paranormal. Secondly, I value my privacy and will not do any media interviews. So where does that leave us?"

"Sorry, but your involvement in the police investigations is already in the public domain. I just want to make it easier for you to tell your story. Now, if you say you are not a psychic, then what have you been doing to aid the police. What information did you provide for them to investigate Senator Salmon?"

"You'll need to talk to the police about that." Amanda decided that this meeting was not going anywhere and was about to leave.

Maxine had other ideas. "I've being delving into your exploits. How about I run some of them by you?" Maxine looked at her notes. "Do you deny being part of the team that plotted the Canberra attack? After getting cold feet you pulled out and betrayed them by tipping off the police? What about this? There are reports that the twins in San Francisco had already reconnected with each other years ago, but they agreed to work with you to fake their reunion. Basically, to score a lucrative TV deal. Did you score a big fee from that one?"

Amanda couldn't believe what she was hearing. "You're way off the mark."

"Am I? What if I put it to you, that you found out Jimmy Pratt had reformed and somehow convinced him to come forward to police and tell them about a fictious mystery man involved in Tonya Manning's murder. And that you illegally gained access to the Salmon's house to plant evidence against the Senator." Maxine sat back gloating as if she had landed several heavy blows.

Amanda was now fuming, but she did her best to compose herself. "You really are something. Nothing you have said is true and in fact it's laughable."

"Is that so? Well, you tell me the truth." Maxine was hoping Amanda would break under the pressure.

Amanda stood up. "Have a nice day. Please don't call me again."

"You'll regret it. I'm not going away." Maxine yelled at Amanda as she left the café.

Since Amanda was already out, she decided to head into her office. It probably meant confronting the waiting media, but she was determined to tell them to leave her alone.

As Amanda neared her office, she noticed a low murmur, a hum. She turned the corner, and the source became obvious. At least a dozen people were hanging around her office. As soon as one person noticed her approaching the whole group leapt into action. Cameras clicked, bright lights shone in her face and then the barrage of questions started.

"Ms Staples are you being paid to help police?"

"Ms Staples have you spoken to Senator Salmon?"

"Ms Staples what details did you provide to the NSW police?"

"Ms Staples have you been inside the Salmon's house?"

The questions came in rapid fire. Amanda kept her head down and pushed her way into her office. Megan unlocked the door and quickly ushered Amanda in, and then locked the door behind her.

"Oh my god! Are you ok?" Megan asked as she fidgeted on the spot. Clearly anxious about the prying eyes and the tapping on the office door.

"I'm a bit shaken, but I have to confront the situation. What about you? I'm sorry you have had to bear the brunt of the media this morning." Amanda directed Megan to her office. At least they would be out of sight from the media outside.

"No. I'm ok. They have been very quiet out there. I wonder how long they are going to hang around?" They both sat down, and Amanda opened her laptop.

"Who knows? I have no experience with this sort of thing." Amanda paused to collect her thoughts. "I met a reporter, Maxine Truman, this morning. It didn't go well."

"What does she want?" Megan moved forward on her chair.

"An exclusive. She said she wants to make it easy to tell my side of the story. But she has already got these wild theories and that I'm a fake." The room was suddenly very quiet.

Megan sat back in her chair. "I don't know any of the details about your psychic skills, but I have known you for a while and there is nothing fake about you."

"Thanks Megan." Amanda smiled. "However, I will correct you. I don't believe I have any psychic abilities. I do see visions, mostly of the future and sometimes of the past, but I have no control over them.

It's not like I can do a psychic reading for someone or channel someone's loved one. It is all very random."

"Ok. So, what are we going to do about the media outside and this Maxine woman?"

Amanda paused and thought about Megan's questions.

"In the short term, I will continue to deny everything. Long term, I have to let the police run with their investigations and see what happens. I've given them a lead, it's up to them. Now, with regard to Maxine Truman. Don't let her in this office and I'll keep putting her off as best I can. We just have to hold our nerve, be patient and wait for this thing to blow over." Amanda didn't sound very confident.

Playing Cat and Mouse

The day dragged on with the occasional disturbance outside Amanda's office reminding them that the media was still there. The office phone and Amanda's mobile were constantly ringing. Amanda resisted answering as many calls as possible, and Megan did her best to put callers off and take messages as required. By the end of the day, they were both exhausted.

Amanda came out to the reception area. "Megan, it's well passed time you were going. What time did you get in?"

"Oh. That's ok. I'm happy to help where I can." She started packing up and gathered her things.

"I suggest you have tomorrow off. I'll won't be coming in. I have a meeting with Tech Corp the day after. So, I'll keep in touch, and I'll see you next week."

"Ok. Time to run the gauntlet." Megan half laughed as she braced herself before heading for the door.

"Bye." Amanda opened the door and Megan quickly slipped out. The waiting media ignored Megan and started shouting at Amanda. She quickly shut the door and shut out the noise.

Amanda started thinking about how she was going to get home and also get away from the waiting media. So far only Maxine Truman had been to her apartment, she was hoping that nobody else had worked out where she lived. Amanda collected her things including her laptop and prepared to leave.

She took a deep breath and opened the door. A barrage of questions hit her. She stopped to give the waiting media one statement. "Hi everyone." The crowd went silent. "I'm sorry, but I cannot comment on current police investigations. You need to talk to the police. I ask that you respect my privacy and leave me alone." Before Amanda could continue, the crowd erupted with questions.

"You can't hide behind the police forever. Tell us your side of the story."

"Ms Staples are you clairvoyant or a medium?"

"Do you want to respond to Senator Salmon's statement that you're a fake?"

The barrage continued, but Amanda was holding firm. "No further comment." She put her head down and pushed her way through the crowd.

Amanda walked as quickly as she could out of the building and down Collins Street. She heard a tram coming along the street and half ran towards the tram stop. Her timing was perfect. She quickly climbed aboard with some of the media in tow. Most had not managed to keep up. The tram was about half full and Amanda remained standing in the centre. A couple of reporters continued to question her, but she zoned out and ignored them. They soon fell silent as many people of the tram were giving them annoying glares.

Amanda knew her preferred stop coming up and she readied herself to exit the tram. She was delighted when she saw a taxi waiting at the nearby taxi stand. Once off the tram, she hurried to the taxi. Climbed in and gave the driver instructions. The driver noticed the accompanying media and sensed the urgency in Amanda's voice. The taxi took off in a hurry, leaving the frustrated media in its wake.

The taxi dropped Amanda off at a tram stop and within 5 minutes she was on a tram heading for her apartment. She was relieved that there was no sign of any reporters. After exiting the tram, she anxiously approached her apartment, hoping that she would not find a horde of people out the front waiting for her. Her spirits lifted when she arrived, and she was alone. It seemed like Maxine Truman was the only reporter to have discovered her address.

Amanda's spirits were lifted even further when she opened the door and was greeted by her pet miniature Schnauzer, Sassy. Pet dogs had this way of lightening your mood every time you meet them.

"Hello, beautiful. I've had a stressful day." Amanda knelt down and gave Sassy a cuddle, before closing the door and heading for the kitchen. She poured herself a wine, kicked of her shoes and slumped into her favourite lounge chair. Sassy immediately jumped up for another cuddle, perhaps sensing her owners need to unwind.

The moment was interrupted by Amanda's phone. "Who is it this time?" The caller ID displayed her closest friend's name. So, Amanda answered with a smile.

"Hi, Jenni."

"Where are you?"

"I just got home."

"Have you seen the news? They've named you as the psychic in the Senator Salmon investigation. They say you had a vision or something." Jenni blurted out her news.

"Thanks. I know."

"Ok, the Senator is calling on you to publicly respond to his accusation that you are a fake."

"Well, I won't be doing that."

"What are you going to do?" Jenni paused.

"I'm not issuing any statement and I've told the media to talk to the police. As for the Senator, he is just trying to deflect the attention away from him."

"Did your phone really capture something about one of the murders?" Jenni wanted to know more.

"Sorry, Jenni. The least I tell anyone is probably for the better. I've given the police information, it's now up to them to use it in their investigations."

"Ok. I understand. It's just a bit spooky you are seeing more visions of the past."

"I still haven't got used to it either. And yes, it does freak me out when a vision is revealed." Amanda took a deep breath before continuing. "Now let's change the topic. How are you? What's been happening?"

"Me. Nothing. I'm heading up a major class action, but nothing exciting like you."

"It's hardly exciting from where I stand. Anyway you, Margo and I need to get together soon."

"Easily done. I'll arrange it with Margo and let you know. Sure, you'll be, ok?" Jenni just wanted reassurance.

"Yes, I'll manage. See you soon. Bye." Amanda immediately turned on the TV to check out the news. Most of the channels were already through their top stories, so Amanda turned her mind to dinner and another glass of wine.

The next day, Amanda hunkered down in her apartment. She kept across the news all day. Most of the channels were saying she was some sort of clairvoyant, but they didn't know how she had gotten into the psychic business. All of them, had now found out about her Emotional Intelligence business and were trying to see if they could make any connection. Margo had been in touch, bringing her up to date with what the media was trying to uncover. She reiterated her warning about Maxine Truman.

Late in the day, Phil Williams called. "Hi Amanda. How are you coping?"

"I'm trying to keep busy on my real job. The media are a pain, but they still haven't found my home address, so I don't feel I'm under siege at home. What's news?"

"The investigation is going at a snail's pace. Sorry, but the Senator has got his solicitors hassling Tony. They want information about you and any other details about the investigation."

"Thanks for the update. When are you in Melbourne again? We should catch up."

"Not in the next couple of weeks. But I'll regularly update you on the case. Got to go. Talk soon. Bye."

"Thanks Phil. Bye." She was hoping the investigation would move along faster, so that things would settle down.

Confrontation

The next day Amanda had a meeting with a potential client. She was meeting with the HR department at Tech Corp to discuss an executive training program in Emotional Intelligence.

She had numerous calls from Maxine Truman, which she had declined, plus other media outlets were still trying to contact her. Margo was still playing interference and shielding Amanda where she could.

Before Amanda left her apartment, she checked outside, and it looked like no one was waiting for her to emerge. She collected her things, said goodbye to Sassy and headed off to her meeting.

Amanda kept a watchful eye for any reporters, but the trip was uneventful, and she entered the building for her meeting feeling relieved. The meeting went well. There was a point in the meeting that the HR manager asked about Amanda's involvement in the NSW police investigation and whether it would impact her ability to deliver her training program in the timeframe they had specified. Amanda reassured the manager that there would be no issues and that she was ready to start once Tech Corp had formally agreed to proceed.

Amanda left the meeting feeling it had been a success and she was looking forward to presenting her updated training program for them. After leaving their reception area, Amanda was shocked to see Maxine Truman waiting in the corridor leading to the lift.

"What are you doing here?" Amanda's rage was building.

"That doesn't matter. I want to talk with you and since you're not answering my calls, I had to see you face to face." Maxine proceeded to pull out a picture from a portfolio, she had under her arm. She showed it to Amanda. "Did you take this picture?" Maxine had a smug look on her face.

"How did you get that?" Amanda was totally caught off guard. The picture was the snapshot taken from her phone of a young Senator Salmon delivering the fatal kick to Tonya Manning. "I am going to report you to the police." Amanda was furious.

"So, you don't deny it. How did you mock-up the picture? It looks pretty authentic." Maxine was on a roll and pushing for any piece of information she could get.

Amanda hesitated and tried to collect her thoughts. Eventually responded in a calm voice. "As I've said before. You need to talk to the police. I have nothing to say to you." Amanda started to push past Maxine when Maxine grabbed her arm.

"You really are a piece of work. You are destroying a man's career and for what. What has Senator Salmon done to you?"

Amanda wrenched her arm away and almost spat back at Maxine. "No comment!"

The pair stood toe to toe in a staring match before Maxine eventually gave in. "I'm publishing an article in tomorrow's papers discrediting you and I'll be on several media shows stating you're a fraud. Just letting you know." Maxine smirked, put the picture back in her portfolio, turned and walked off.

Amanda wanted to reply with something cutting but couldn't think of anything in that moment. So, she decided to video Maxine as she turned and walked away. Amanda turned for phone on and followed Maxine along the corridor. Maxine disappeared from the screen as she rounded a bend in the corridor. As Amanda turned the corner, she was surprised to see the corridor had changed. She got the feeling she was now in a hospital. Nurses and other people were busy going in and out of rooms along the corridor. Amanda stopped and was standing outside a room with the door open. She pointed her phone into the room. It shows a person in a bed, seemingly asleep connected to several machines. Amanda nervously edged her way into the room. Even though the persons had lost their hair, Amanda recognized the patient as Maxine Truman.

Amanda jumped as she heard someone entering the room. A doctor and a nurse appeared next to Maxine's bed. Amanda quickly glanced at her watch through her phone. It indicated that she was three months in the future.

"She will need another treatment of chemo. The cancer is aggressive, and I'd like to hit it hard." The Doctor was looking at a medical chart.

The nurse moved around the bed and adjusted Maxine's pillow, and she commented. "It's sad, she didn't get tested earlier."

"Yes, even one week would have made a substantial difference." The doctor added. Amanda was shocked and wanted to check the date again. She moved her watch into view then the video stopped with a snapshot of Maxine flanked by her doctor and the nurse. Her watch clearly displayed in the foreground.

Amanda took a deep breath and looked around. She realised she was still standing in the corridor, not a hospital ward. She looked at the picture again and realised she needed to find Maxine Truman and fast. Amanda hurried to the lift, but Maxine was already gone. Once she was out of the building, Amanda realised, she had Maxine's number in her phone. She pressed the call button and waited.

Changing minds

"So, you do want to talk?" Maxine answered.

"Yes. I've had a change of heart. Where are you?" Amanda wanted to meet as soon as possible.

"I'm heading for my car. I need to put some more money in the meter, then I can meet you."

Amanda looked around before replying. "There is a café across the road from the Tech Corp building we were just in. I'll meet you there."

"Ok. I'll be there shortly."

All sorts of things were running through Amanda's mind as she waited in the café. How does she convince a sceptic like Maxine that her picture in the hospital ward is potentially her future? How much does she tell Maxine about her phone and visions? Her thoughts were interrupted when Maxine arrived and sat opposite her. There was an uneasy silence between them.

Amanda still had the picture displayed on her phone. So, she messaged it to Maxine's number. Maxine's phone sounded a notification.

"Please have a look at your phone." Amanda broke the silence.

Maxine collected her phone from her bag and opened the message. Her eyes widened as she started to comprehend what she was looking at. "Are you trying to threaten me?" Was her first reaction.

"No. I'm showing you a potential vision of the future. You can see the date on my watch." Amanda raised her hand with her watch to illustrate that the watch in the picture was the same as on Amanda's wrist.

Maxine did a double take of the watch and the picture. "Is this another fake? How did you create this?" Amanda could see the doubt on Maxine's face.

"I am going to tell you something and I hope you will keep it confidential, but in the end, you are a reporter, and I suppose you will do what you will." Amanda paused to gather her thoughts.

"As I have said before. I don't consider myself a psychic. However, since a certain incident earlier this year, I have been able to snap photos on my phone of the future and sometimes of the past. I don't know how or why it happens and I certainly cannot control what I see. It started before the Canberra terrorist attack, which led to my cooperation with the AFP. I have helped in the prevention of a murder. Helped find a missing hiker. Reunited the twins in San Francisco to name just a few of the visions I have had. I was asked, by my AFP contact, to assist in the Bondi Gay-hate crimes investigation and uncovered a mystery third person involved in a murder. My phone recorded an incident that took place some 30 years ago. The picture you showed me is no fake, nor is the one in the message I just sent you."

Maxine's expression had changed to one of uncertainty, but also of some willingness to try and understand what was been presented to her. "Do you have proof?"

"Well, that's the thing. My phone actually starts with a video, and I see a vision of the future or the past and then at a critical moment my phone takes a snapshot and the video ends. The photo is only available to view while I keep it open. Once I close it or even return to my gallery the snapshot is gone. However, I have discovered recently, that if I immediately send the photo as an attachment in a message, the receiver gets a copy which can be kept. Thus, the photo on your phone."

Maxine was still trying to comprehend what she was hearing. "So, this is nothing to do with you being psychic. You're telling me it's all about the phone." She paused. "Can anyone use it and see a vision?"

"I don't think so. Some of my friends have tried watching over my shoulder, but nothing paranormal happens. I haven't given the phone to anyone to try on their own, and the AFP phone analysis unit found nothing unusual about it after the terrorist attack."

Maxine was looking more closely at the photo. "This is supposedly me in the future. How do you know when it will occur?"

"You can see my watch there, with the date. I realised I can move my watch into view, and it shows the date at the time of the video or photo."

"Ok. Sure, you mentioned the watch before. Sorry, I'm still not sure what I'm seeing or meant to believe.

"In videos of the future, I can hear the sound of what is happening. In your video the doctor and nurse you see were discussing your case." Amanda wondered whether she should tell Maxine what was said or not.

"What did they say?" Maxine interrupted her thoughts.

"That you should have been tested earlier. Even one week would have made a substantial difference." Amanda waited to see Maxine's reaction.

"Oh my god!" Maxine's face went pale. "I cancelled a check-up with a skin specialist that was due today. I have a mole that has been troubling me."

"Did you rebook?" Amanda could see Maxine starting to worry.

"No. I'm very busy and was going to try for next month."

"You need to go today. Tell them it's an emergency and that you really are worried. This is no joke." Amanda was trying to impress the urgency on Maxine.

Maxine stared at Amanda searching for answers. "I'm not sure I understand any of this. I know I don't believe in clairvoyance, but something makes me want to believe you or maybe this photo. Can I ever change the future?"

"I think you can. I have seen visions and then altered the future by acting on the knowledge of what I have seen. Please call your specialist now."

"Okay. I'll actually go there now and make them see me. I'll call you later. Thank you." Maxine and Amanda both stood up. There was an awkward pause between them, then Maxine hurried out of the café.

Amanda heard nothing for the rest of the day or evening. She did speak to both Jenni and Margo to update them on what had happened with Maxine. They were both shocked and hoped for the best.

The next morning Amanda was back in her office. Only a few reporters were outside her office to greet her. She gave them the usual response. "Please talk to the police. I have nothing to say."

She had just settled at her desk when her phone rang, it was from Maxine.

Amanda answered with a deal of trepidation. "Hi Maxine. How are you?" She cringed as she waited for a reply.

"Hi Amanda. Yes, I'm ok. I eventually convinced them to let me see the specialist. I'm in hospital right now."

"What?" Amanda was preparing herself for the worst.

"It's ok. They operated late yesterday afternoon and removed a melanoma. They think they got it all and we are now just waiting on the lab results. The doctor is coming around in the next hour. All indications so far, are that they got it in time." Amanda heard a sigh of relieve from the of end.

Maxine then continued. "Thank you so much for sharing your photo with me. I didn't believe anything about you or your visions, but now

I must say I have a different view. Sorry, I couldn't cancel my article in the papers, but I have cancelled my media interviews, and I intend to publish a retraction in the papers as soon as possible. Plus, I have a little bit of influence with some of the other reporters. I'll see if they can give you some space and wait to see where the police investigation leads. Once again, I can't thank you enough. Hope we can catch up soon."

"I hope so too. Good luck with the results. Bye." Amanda finally let herself breathe. It seemed like she had been holding her breath the whole time.

Megan popped her head in the door. "Hi. There was a call from Tech Corp while you were on the phone. They are ready to proceed with the training and want you to come in and finalise the contract."

"Great. Let's do this." Amanda was buoyed by the news and felt that some sort of normality was returning to her life.

The Whistleblower

Got to get away

The media attention had not abated and now that they knew Amanda's home address there was a constant media presence either at her office or her apartment. Maxine Truman's diagnosis was good. Amanda had visited Maxine to check on her condition and treatment. The lab results had come back positive, but her doctor believed they had removed the entire melanoma and so far, there was no sign of any spread. Maxine apologised for the media and said that in time things would die down. Amanda was not so sure. A friendship was starting to grow between them.

The investigation into Tonya Manning's murder and Senator Salmon's involvement was continuing. The Senator was still in complete denial and continued to accuse Amanda of being a fake. Sections of the media didn't want this story to fade away and made getting Amanda's side of the story a priority.

Amanda arrived home after another busy day. She pushed her way through the reporters, not responding to their barrage of questions. Once inside she was relieved to have Sassy greet her, with her normal excitement.

"Yes. It's great to see you too, beautiful." She gave Sassy a cuddle and headed for the kitchen. Before she knew it, she had a glass of wine in her hand and had slumped down into her favourite lounge chair. "I'm getting sick of this." She said to Sassy as she jumped up to join Amanda. "We need to get away. How about we go and visit Buster?" Sassy didn't react, she was just happy with having her ear scratched. Buster was Amanda's Uncle Alf and Auntie Mary's pet kelpie. They had a farm near Griffith in NSW. Amanda had spent many of her childhood holidays with her Uncle and Auntie and she loved the farm.

Amanda grabbed her phone and spent the next half hour arranging her trip. First, she called Auntie Mary, who was delighted to have her come and stay. Next was Jenni and Margo to let them know she would be away for about a week. They both agreed it was a good idea and told her to rest up while away. Amanda called Megan to inform her and discussed her schedule to determine who she needed to call and what could be postponed. There were no immediate deadlines, so the timing was good. Amanda advised Megan that the office would be closed and that she could work from home. Lastly, she called Phil Williams. Phil was sorry that the NSW police investigation was dragging on and agreed that getting away would be a good idea. As always, he would keep her up to date with the investigation and was always available if she needed assistance.

Amanda immediately felt like a heavy weight had been lifted from her shoulders. She settled back into the lounge, for tonight, she would relax then early tomorrow she would pack and head off for Griffith.

Overnight, Amanda started to think about how she would evade the media. It didn't help her to get to sleep, but in the morning, she had an idea. She wanted to make them believe that she was going to her work as normal. She packed her car, which was in the underground parking lot, beneath her apartment. Dressed in a work outfit, she left by the front door and wished the waiting reporters good morning. She headed for her normal tram stop. It wasn't long before the tram arrived, and Amanda was on her way. Some reporters joined her on the tram, others scrambled to their cars and headed for her office. The reporters didn't hassle Amanda too much on the tram, not wanting to make a scene. Amanda alighted at her normal stop but headed straight to the nearest taxi stand. Catching the following media off guard. There was a taxi waiting and she grabbed it. The reporters were left frustrated in her wake. She instructed the driver to take her home. However, instead of being dropped out in front of her apartment, Amanda instructed the driver to go around to the lane at the back, which leads the parking lot entrance. There was a side door, which Amanda used to enter the building. She went to her apartment, quickly changed into some comfortable traveling clothes, grabbed Sassy and headed for her car.

Amanda clipped Sassy into her harness, started the car and exited the parking lot. To her relieve there was no sign of any reporters. She had made a clean get away. It was a full day's drive to Griffith with stops every couple of hours or so. Sassy travelled well in the car and enjoyed sniffing around during their stops.

Familiar Surrounds

Amanda's Auntie Mary was at home when she arrived. Mary was in her early 70s. She was a hardy sort with her grey hair pulled into a bun. She had a big smile on her face as she came out of the homestead to greet Amanda.

"Hi Auntie." Amanda called from the car as she exited.

"Amanda, it's great to see you. You made good time." Amanda had unhooked Sassy and the Schnauzer excitedly greeted Mary. "You remember me, Sassy?" Mary gave Sassy a pat.

"Is Uncle Alf here?" Amanda asked as the two warmly embraced.

"No. He is out checking on some sheep in the North paddock. He and Buster will be back soon." Mary helped Amanda with her bags and then added. "So, are you going to tell me about this psychic business?"

"It has been a long drive. Got to be time for a wine." Amanda smiled. "Then we can chat."

Mary showed Amanda to her room, even though Amanda knew the way. They chatted about the weather, farming and nothing in particular until they settled on the back veranda with a glass of wine each.

"I don't consider myself a psychic, but recently I have been having visions of the future and even sometimes of the past. I can't control them, and I still don't know why they are happening."

"Well, it's not hereditary. I don't know of any clairvoyant in the family." Mary was into ancestry and knew the family history very well. Mary paused for a moment and gazed at Amanda. "You actually had a vision of this Senator kicking the victim?"

"Yes. What's really freaky, is that it happened over 30 years ago. The Senator was only about 18 or 19. Of course he is still denying it was him, but the police are slowly piecing together more evidence against him."

"What about the reunion of the twins in San Francisco, that must have been emotional? How did you find the missing twin?" Mary was showing real interest in Amanda's psychic exploits.

"It's a long story and I'd prefer not to think about all that right now. I've come here to get away from all the attention."

"That's ok. I get the hint. I'll also tell your uncle not to broach the topic." Mary was a bit disappointed, but she sensed Amanda's reluctance and resigned herself to leave the topic alone for now.

They heard a car pull up on the gravel driveway and Sassy pricked up her ears. "That will be your uncle." Mary presumed.

It wasn't long before Buster came trotting around the corner of the homestead, tail wagging. While Buster and Sassy went through the usual dog greetings, Alf came around the corner. His crusty old face broke into a big grin when he saw Amanda.

"Great to see you, Amanda." The two warmly embraced.

"You too, Uncle."

"Let me get out of these dirty overalls and boots. Oh, and I've got something for you." Alf went in the back door and returned a short while later having changed. Mary had poured a third glass of wine ready for Alf. He sat down with them and gave Amanda a bottle of fortified wine liqueur.

"It's a local Tokay, but the label says 'Topaque', because apparent the European Union doesn't like us calling it Tokay and so in Australia they are being renamed as Topaque, which sounds like tow-pack-ee." They all had a bit of a laugh at Alf's pronunciation.

"That's lovely Uncle. Thank you." Amanda lent over and gave her uncle a peck on the cheek.

"So, what brings you back to see us?" Alf started and Mary immediately interrupted.

"Alf. I told you Amanda was coming for a break, to get away from all the fuss."

"Sure. I forgot. It seems to be happening more these days." Alf had a bit of a chuckle.

"Well, my business is going well, and I've completed the draft of my new book. Still a way to go before it will be ready for publishing, but I'm happy with it so far. How are things on the farm?" Amanda wanted to direct the conversation away from her.

Alf sighed. "The usual. It never rains when you want it, and then it pours. The flooding around NSW has been disastrous but so far, out here, it hasn't been too bad. We are over twice the monthly average already for this month, but it hasn't been as wet as 1971. Lambing has been good this year, but fly strike is going to be really bad." Alf looked down at his weathered hands. They all went silent for what seemed ages. Amanda decided to broach a sensitive subject about the couple's future.

"Have you decided what to do with the farm yet?"

"No. Your Auntie and I are still procrastinating about when I should retire, and with no kids, I suppose we'll just sell up and be done with it." Amanda could hear the emotion in Alf's voice.

"Alf's been on the farm all his life. So, it's hard." Mary added, not daring to look at Amanda. "I suppose it's time I went and started dinner. You two can finish the wine." Mary grabbed her glass and hurried inside.

Exploitation

Amanda and her uncle continued with idle chit chat while they finished the bottle of wine. Somehow the topic drifted to the last orange harvest and fruit growing in general. Alf had pulled out all his orange trees some time ago. He now just focused on sheep and cereal crops.

"It was heart breaking to see many of the orange growers having fruit rot on the ground because of the lack of seasonal workers to pick the fruit. The future doesn't look any better for the stone fruit growers either." Alf lamented.

Amanda commented. "I know the Seasonal Worker Program, run by the government, is struggling to get migrant workers. Do you know if the exploitation of temporary migrant workers is still happening?"

"I don't think things have changed that much. Things improve when there is a bit of media attention, but with so few workers, those unscrupulous labour hire contractors are bound to be active."

At that moment, Mary called from inside the house, saying dinner was nearly ready. During dinner the conversation continued about the plight of farming, as their future weighed heavily on Alf and Mary. Alf finally conceded that selling up and retiring to the northern beaches of NSW was firming as one of their options. Amanda sensed the reluctance by the couple to sell up, as the farm was all they had known.

The next morning, Amanda found Mary in the kitchen. She had heard Alf leave earlier with the dogs. Sassy was going to have an adventurous day out on the farm with Buster. The local paper was on the table and the front page featured an article about migrant worker exploitation. They had information from an anonymous whistleblower about the exploitation of migrants without valid visas, commonly known as undocumented workers.

Mary looked over Amanda's shoulder and commented. "That's one thing we are relieved about, not having to source workers for the harvest. Over the years it has become very messy. In the old days it was standard practice to pay pickers by the bin filled. It was tough work, but the pickers seemed to be hardier then. No one seemed to complain, but these days pickers expect an hourly rate with benefits. So, some farmers look for alternatives and that's where these labour hire contractors thrive."

Amanda didn't comment. She didn't want to get into any argument with her Auntie about worker's rights and fare pay for a day's work. Amanda went to the pantry to get some cereal for breakfast.

Mary changed the topic, as she put the jug on for another coffee. "So, what are your plans for today?"

"How about I take you into town for a proper coffee and I can just check out the town. See if anything has changed. You can give me the tour. Maybe do some window shopping." Amanda smiled.

"Ok. I'd better get changed into something a bit more presentable for town." She looked down at her apron and chuckled.

The Agent and Informant

Amanda and Mary did some window shopping. Mary picked up some groceries and collected the mail from the post office. Then they settled into some seats at a roadside café to enjoy a proper coffee.

A man walked up to their table that Mary recognised. "Hello Matt. How are you today?"

"Hi Mrs G. Yeah, I'm good and you?" Matt Coulson was in his 40s and dressed in semi business attire.

"Matt, this is my niece, Amanda. She is up from Melbourne. Amanda, Matt's family own the farm next to us. You two played together as toddlers when you visited." Mary smiled.

Amanda became a bit uncomfortable because she couldn't remember anything about Matt.

"That was a long time ago, Auntie. Matt wouldn't remember me." Amanda tried to deflect back to Matt.

"Oh, I remember. You used to throw dirt at me." Matt was smirking at Amanda's awkwardness. "But you're right it was a long time ago. You here for a while?"

"Not sure yet. Maybe a week." Amanda smiled back.

"Well, enjoy your stay. See you around Mrs G. Bye, Amanda." Matt strolled off.

"Bye." Mary lowered her voice and commented to Amanda. "Matt works for an agency that works with the government in the Seasonal Worker Program. His older brother, Harry has taken over the family farm."

Amanda just nodded her head in acknowledgement. She then leaned forward and commented. "That was a bit embarrassing, I really don't remember him." They both had a laugh.

Later that afternoon, back on the farm, Amanda decided to take a walk. It was a glorious sunny day in the high-twenties and Amanda wanted to have a look around the property. She said goodbye to her Auntie and headed out the back door. She wondered where her uncle was and how Sassy was coping.

She knew the layout of the property and headed out along one of the lanes, which criss-crossed the farm. After about half an hour, she came to a gate on the boundary of the property, which opened onto a dirt backroad. She went through and knew that if she turned right along the backroad, it would lead her to the north paddock. Maybe Alf was out there.

It was such a beautiful day and with all the local birds chirping, she decided to get her phone out and video the surrounding country as the road wound its way through some old red gums. The video showed a car approaching from the other direction. Amanda was immediately surprised as the phone had no sound. She pressed the side buttons, but it had no effect. The car came to a stop in front of her and she recognised Matt Coulson sitting alone in the driver seat. Amanda jumped as another car came into view. It had come from the other direction and surprised her. It was a rusty, dinted old Ute. The utility stopped in front of Matt's car and a middle-aged woman climbed out. Matt joined her and they engaged in what seemed like an energetic discussion. The woman was fidgeting the whole time and Amanda assumed she was very nervous about something. The video stopped displaying a snapshot of the two facing each other, deep in conversation.

Amanda commented to herself. "I wonder what that was all about?" She looked around and of course there were no cars to be seen. Amanda assumed the meeting must had taken place in the past, as there was no sound. She put her phone away and continued walking, but she couldn't stop thinking about what they were talking about.

Amanda found her uncle and the dogs at one of the large hay sheds in the north paddock. He was stacking some hay bales onto his Ute.

"That looks like hard work." Amanda commented as she approached her uncle.

"Yeah, it's not getting any easier." Amanda grabbed one end of the bale, that Alf was lifting and helped him toss it into the Ute. "Thanks. That's the last one. Did you walk from the homestead?" Alf asked a bit surprised.

"Yep. It's such a glorious day. I needed to get outside." Sassy was already at Amanda side, excited to see her. She knelt down and gave Sassy a pat. "How has she been going?" She asked ruffling her ears.

Alf lent on the Ute looking tied. "She really loves it out here with Buster." Buster was climbing in and amongst the hay bales sniffing around for something. "And I think he enjoys her company. I've finished out here. You want a lift home?"

"Thanks."

Amanda squeezed into the passenger's seat with Sassy on her lap, while Buster jumped onto the back of the Ute. Along the back roads, it only took about fifteen minutes, and they were back at the homestead. Alf had commented that the bales were for some sheep out in a paddock west of the homestead. He would drop them off tomorrow morning.

It was nearing dusk. Amanda, her uncle and auntie sat on the back veranda and enjoyed a glass of wine, chatting about their day. They were interrupted when Amanda's phone rang. It was Phil Williams. Amanda stood up, excused herself and answered the call.

"Hi Phil. How are things?"

"Yeah, good. Hope you are enjoying your break. However, I have some news."

"Ok."

"Some fibres, collected from Tonya Manning's body, had been stored with all the other evidence from her case and had never really been analysed. Thirty years ago, technology wasn't that great. Well, in light of your new evidence, the police have been going back over every piece of evidence they have. To their surprise, they found some DNA and got it tested."

"That's amazing. What did they find?" Amanda was getting excited.

"The interesting thing is Senator Salmon agreed to give a DNA sample, believing that after 30 years there would be nothing for him to worry about. In fact, he wanted to demonstrate he was confident of his innocence. Well, the DNA came back as a match."

"What? You're joking?" Amanda was elated.

"No. Plus, they have been able to match the Senator's DNA to two other unsolved cases from the same period. They are confident now that they can prosecute a case against him."

"That is amazing. I have been staying off the grid out here on the farm. I suppose it's all over the news?" Amanda was dreading the potential increase in attention.

"Yep. It's the lead story on all the main media channels. But, so far, they are not reporting much about your involvement. It's all about the DNA."

"Tony and his team must be over the moon?"

"Yes, Tony is very relieved and asked me to pass on his gratitude. Anyway, I've got to go. Call me when you get back to Melbourne. Bye."

"Thanks for calling, Phil. Goodbye." Amanda had a big smile on her face as she returned to her uncle and auntie.

"You look very pleased. What was that all about?" Mary asked.

"Amazingly, the NSW police have found old DNA evidence that's a match to the Senator. Apparently, it's all over the news." Amanda was about to sit down, but Mary jumped up and headed inside.

"Come on. We can catch the news while I prepare dinner." She had a cheeky smirk on her face.

Amanda conceded that she was going to hear about this for the next couple of days, so she may as well hear it firsthand. "Come on uncle. We had better do as we are told." Amanda held the door open as Alf eased himself out of his seat and headed inside.

The news outlets were reporting how shocked everyone was, that the newly elected Senator could have been such a hateful young man. Luckily for Amanda, her role as the psychic barely got a mention. It was all about the DNA discovery and match.

"Well, you must be relieved. You didn't get a mention." Mary commented from the kitchen.

"Yes. I hope this will mean the media attention will die down. I can get back to concentrating on my business." Amanda was feeling a sense of relief.

The next morning, Amanda went into Griffith, to run a few errands for her auntie, while Mary was visiting an elderly relative in a nursing home.

After dropping Mary off, Amanda parked her car in the main street. As she looked around, she realised she had parked outside the Seasonal Worker Program office, were she presumed Matt Coulson worked. She thought back to the recording and snapshot on her phone of Matt meeting someone out on the back road. Suddenly she had this pressing urge to use her phone. While she sat in her car, she grabbed her phone and started the video. She pointed her phone at the office, and immediately the door opened. Matt Coulson was coming out of the office. Amanda heard the door open and close through her phone and knew that this had to be in the future. Matt turned away from Amanda's position in the car and started walking along the street. Amanda noticed a person coming into the video from across the street. It was a tall, burly looking man in his 50s. He stepped in front of Matt making him stop in his tracks.

"You bastard! Stop spreading lies about my business." The man shouted at Matt.

Matt was taken aback by the man's viciousness. "I don't know what you're talking about. Excuse me." Matt started to walk around the man. The man responded by grabbing Matt's arm and stopping him.

"I run a legitimate contracting business. Just because you think you work for the government doesn't mean you can stick your grubby nose in my business." The man was ranting.

Matt pulled his arm out of the man's grip and started to assert himself in reply. "Look. My job is to help farmers and migrant workers, not exploit vulnerable people. I don't know how you run your business, but if you treat people the right way and pay them what they allowed by law, then you have nothing to worry about." Matt turned and walked away.

"You Wanka. Stay out of my business and stop feeding the paper lies." The video stopped as the man turned towards Amanda. The snapshot showed Matt walking away in the background, and in the foreground, facing Amanda, the man with an angry red-looking face.

Amanda looked up from her phone and there was no one in front of Matt's office. She then berated herself for not checking her watch through her phone. She had no idea how far in the future the confrontation would take place. She then started to wonder. '*Who was the angry man?*'

Tragedy and Justice

Amanda immediately thought she should go and warn Matt, but then how would she explain her visions. She was conflicted. One thing she decided to do was get todays local newspaper. Clearly, something had spurred the angry man into action.

Amanda grabbed a newspaper from a local shop and sure enough the glaring headline said.

"DODGY CONTRACTOR REVEALED – WHISTLEBLOWER TELLS ALL."

Amanda returned to her car and read through the article. The whistleblower outlined how undocumented workers paid hefty fees to "dodgy" migration worker contract agents, for them to organise their visa. Many of these migrants thought they were entering the Seasonal Worker Program and were promised they would get a well-paid job – only to arrive and discover they're on a tourist visa with no right to work. Then the unscrupulous labour hire contractor would, in some cases, forcibly take them to the regions, where they were forced to work illegally on farms to repay their debt.

The anonymous whistleblower apparently named the contract agency "Nu Pickers Co-op" as the main culprit in the Griffith area. A spokesperson for the Seasonal Worker Program was quoted as saying. "These migrant workers are subjected to exorbitant prices for accommodation, wage theft, unlawful deductions and other horrible examples of abuse." Amanda presumed that was Matt.

An Australian government spokesperson was also quoted as saying there was, a "zero tolerance" approach to worker exploitation, and workers are briefed before departure and on arrival in Australia to ensure they understand their visa entitlements, but the exploitation continues.

Amanda took a deep breath to absorb everything she had read and then realised it was time she was meant to pick up Mary. She put the paper aside and headed off to collect Mary from the nursing home. She apologised to Mary, as she picked her up, for being a bit late.

"That's ok. Get everything done?" Mary was referring to the errands Amanda was attending to for her.

"Yes. No problems. I lost track of time reading the main story in the paper." Amanda motioned to the paper on the back seat as she drove off. Mary had a quick glance.

"Oh, that. Yes, I read it while I was in the nursing home. It's horrible and gives us farmers a bad name, because people think we are the ones abusing the system."

"I suppose you and Uncle Alf are happy to be out of the fruit growing business?" Amanda suggested.

"Exactly. But we never experienced anything like this in our time." Mary and Amanda both descended into their own thoughts and the rest of the drive home was in relative silence.

Back at the homestead the conversation continued about the exploitation of pickers and what could be done about it. Of course, Alf and Mary sided with the poor farmers trying to get their harvest picked. They did concede that the governments Seasonal Worker

Program was probably the best regulated program available, even with its shortcomings.

The next morning, Amanda decided to go for a run. She had been a bit lax during her stay so far and felt a good 5km run would be good for her. She was up early and said goodbye to Sassy and Buster before heading off along one of the back roads. She would go out for approximately 2.5km and turn around.

Nearing the turnaround point, Amanda realised she had returned to the place where she had videoed the meeting between Matt and the woman. She stopped, grabbed her phone from its pouch and paused her fitness app. Next thing she was turning on the video again to see if anything else would happen.

Immediate the scenery on the screen changed. It was still a back road but not what Amanda could see in front of her. The other thing that was different was the woman, from the previous vision, was already there. She was standing, leaning on the front of her rusty, dinted old Ute. Once again, there was no sound. Amanda remembered to move her watch into view, and she checked the date. It was about a week ago. A black car came into view and stopped in front of the woman. It was not the car Matt Coulson had used. The woman seemed to panic and rushed to get into her car. A person stepped out of the black car levelled a gun and shot the woman in the back. The video stopped and Amanda looked at the snapshot in horror. It clearly showed the woman falling forward, as a result of being shot in the back. There was the flash of the gun discharging and the person holding the gun was none other than the big angry man that had confronted Matt Coulson yesterday.

Amanda looked up from her phone and was relieved to see no one on the road. Her heart was pounding. She slowed her breathing to compose herself and then sent the snapshot in a message to Phil Williams at the AFP. She didn't know what else she could do at that moment.

Her phone rang immediately. "Hi Amanda. Where are you? What's happened?" Phil sounded concerned.

"I'm ok. I just had a vision of the past. As you can see a woman was shot. I don't know if she is dead, and I don't know the location of the shooting." Amanda felt useless.

"Ok. Calm down. Are you still in Griffith?"

"Yes."

"Alright. You will have to go to the police but wait for me. I'll come straight out there. I'll catch a flight today. I'll also send the snapshot to Tony Pirelli. We are going to need support from within the NSW police. He will back us up due to your work on the Tonya Manning case." He paused for a moment, then asked again. "Amanda, are you ok?"

"I think so. It's always scary seeing a vision on my phone, especially when its violent. I'll wait the hear from you once you arrive in Griffith."

"Good. I'll see you soon. Bye." Phil was gone. Amanda looked at her phone. The snapshot had gone and the video. Well, that was of an empty country back road.

Later that afternoon, Amanda and Phil reported to the local police station and asked for the duty Sergeant. Phil had printed the snapshot and briefed Tony Pirelli. The Sergeant was alarmed when he was shown the picture and ushered Amanda and Phil into one of the stations interview rooms. He left them there alone while he rang Tony Pirelli on advice from Phil.

When he returned, he had another constable with him.

"Ok. Detective Pirelli highly recommends you and your psychic abilities Ms Staples. We have identified both parties in the photo. At this stage I would rather not name names. The victim, however, is a migrant worker and we believe she had been providing information anonymously regarding alleged "dodgy" migration worker contract agents. In particular, the Nu Pickers Co-op. The person, seemingly firing the gun, is one of the partners in the Nu Pickers Co-op."

Amanda interrupted the Sergeant. "I think it's pretty clear from the photo he is firing the gun."

"Well. That has yet to be proven." He counted. "Now, so far, the victim has not been located, but we have launched a full-scale search of the district. Off course, the picture doesn't give us a location and there are many back roads."

"What about the big angry man." Amanda again interrupted much to the Sergeants apparent annoyance.

"Ms Staples. We cannot arrest a person based on a vision. Even though it is damming."

Phil chipped in. "What about searching his car and premises?"

"Well, yes. I was coming to that. Based on advice from Detective Pirelli, and other recent events involving migrant workers, we are seeking several warrants. But that takes time. For now, it's a wait and see, if we discover a body and a magistrate agrees to our requests. Then we can proceed."

The meeting finished with Amanda feeling frustrated and a little apprehensive about her vision and whether they would find a body. Phil was more upbeat and said the police had to follow due process.

Phil joined Amanda at the homestead that evening. Alf and Mary wanted to know all the details and as the evening dragged on, Mary insisted that Phil stay the night. They had plenty of room. In the end, he graciously accepted. Tony had called Phil during the evening but had nothing new to add. It all depended on the search for the woman's body.

The next morning dragged on slowly. The local and national news outlets provided full coverage of the story, but the police remained tight lipped about the details. The search was expanded, and more people were brought in to help. Around midday, news broke of a discovery.

"Come quick. There is breaking news." Mary called out from the lounge room. Amanda, Phil and Alf all hurried back from where they had been, either spending time of their phone, or quietly pondering possible outcomes, or doing little odd jobs around the house.

They all watch the news presenter as she announced that a car had been found and it matched the description of the woman's Ute. It was on a back road 10km west of the town. No body had been found yet and sniffer dogs had arrived to assist in the search. Amanda slumped into a chair and breathed a sigh of relief. Her vision had been real.

Phil's phone rang. "Hello. Yes." Everyone turned to watch and wait to hear what was happening. "Okay. That's great, but tragic news. Thanks for the update. Bye." Phil looked around the room.

"That was Tony. They have found the woman's body. One of the sniffer dogs found her. She was in a shallow grave about 50 metres from the road. In light of the discovery, the warrants have been approved and police are currently acting on them. They have kept this all quite for the moment and Tony expects there will be a formal media conference later today." Phil smiled at Amanda. "Looks like your visions have been vindicated again. It's a great result."

Amanda half smiled. "Yes, but it didn't save that woman's life."

In the media conference later that day, the police didn't mention anything about psychic visions or Amanda's involvement, much to her relief.

The next day Amanda and Phil departed for their homes, thanking Alf and Mary. Amanda said she hoped to be back soon to have a more relaxing break.

What is the Point?

Good to be Home:

Amanda was glad to be home. She was also very happy to notice there were no waiting reporters gathered outside her apartment. Sassy was also happy to be home, being on the farm with Buster the kelpie had been exhausting for a miniature Schnauzer.

After unpacking and giving Sassy something to eat, Amanda rang her friend Jenni. "Hi Jenni. I'm sorry I haven't called in the last couple of days. The last few days have been a bit hectic."

"That's ok. I knew you were trying to chill out while away." Jenni paused before asking. "Did you have something to do with that shooting in Griffith? I'm not implying that you did any shooting, but did you see a vision?"

"I know what you mean. Yes, I did have a vision, and it led to finding that poor woman and hopefully it will help convict the person responsible."

"So, not a holiday. Well, back here things have been dull, and boring. We need to go out for dinner somewhere. I'll contact Margo and arrange it. Any preferences?"

"Somewhere quiet. So, we can chat without having to shout." Amanda suggested.

"Ok. I'll find somewhere classy. We can then dress up. Leave it to me."

"Alright. Great to talk. Bye." Talking to Jenni had put a smile on Amanda's face. Next, she called, Margo.

"Hi Margo." Before she could continue, Margo pounced.

"Are you trying to make my job of protecting you harder. The media attention has just started to ease off and then, I presume you have gone and solve another murder."

Amanda had to laugh. "Margo, you know I can't control the visions. The good thing is, other than the police, no one knows I had anything to do with the case."

"That may be so, but people leak stuff to the media all the time. Anyway, good to have you back. I have setup a meeting for a review of your draft."

"Thanks. I just spoke to Jenni. She will contact you to organise a dinner out."

"I've got a text message already. I know just the place. I'll call her shortly. Now, you keep your head down and stay out of trouble. See you soon. Ciao."

"Thanks, Margo. Bye." Amanda had one more call to make.

"Hi Depindar."

"Hi Amanda, you're back. How was your trip?"

"Eventful." Amanda had a little chuckle. "I'll tell you all about it tomorrow. Will you be right for a run in the morning?"

"Yes. I missed our morning jog. I've got to go but can chat then."

"Cheers. Bye." Amanda was happy things were returning to normal.

On her way to work, the next morning, Amanda had a suspicious feeling that she was being watched or that someone was following her. It was frustrating because she didn't really see anyone. Perhaps she was being a bit paranoid, after all the media attention. She wasn't sure but it made her feel uncomfortable.

Megan, her assistant, arrived at 9am and Amanda shared details of her Griffith trip over a coffee. Once they got down to business, Megan confirmed that the EQ training with Tech Corp executives was all arranged and starting later that week.

Alarming

The rest of the day went very quickly. Amanda checked in with Margo again regarding her book draft review and who was going to be attending. She also did some planning for her next podcast. Megan left about 4pm and Amanda continued working to 5:30pm.

She left her office and headed home taking her normal tram. Amanda got off the tram at her stop and walked a little way along the road before stopping at a T-intersection. The lights changed and Amanda was about to start walking across the road when a car came speeding through the red light fishtailing as it turned through the intersection. Amanda had to jump back as the rear of the car veered very close and could have hit her if she hadn't moved back. The car sped away with tyre and exhaust smoke billowing into the air.

At that moment, Amanda's phone rang. She was breathless as she fumbled around in her handbag trying to find her phone. Finally, she pulled it out and saw the caller was Phil Williams.

"Amanda. Are you ok?" Phil blurted down the phone.

"Aaah! A little shaken but ok I suppose. Why are you calling?" She was still flustered.

"Your alarm went off. The AFP tracking app on your phone sent a call to the control centre and they rang me."

"I didn't activate the alarm. My phone was in my bag." Amanda was confused.

"Ok. You sound a little breathless. Did something just happen?"

"Well, yes. A car nearly hit me as I was about to cross the road." Amanda was starting to calm down as she looked around surveying the intersection.

"That must have been scary. Do you think it was deliberate?" Phil was curious.

"What? I don't know. I didn't take any notice of who was in the car. It just appeared from nowhere and ran the red light."

"Interesting that your phone activated the alarm on its own. I think that's the second time it's done that. That phone is pretty special."

The traffic lights changed again, Amanda proceeded to cross the road with caution and continued on her way home.

Phil continued as she walked. "I was meaning to call you today anyway. I have some not so good news from Griffith." Amanda interrupted Phil. "Can it wait a moment. I'm nearly home and the noise out here is making it hard to hear you. I'll call back in a couple of minutes. Ok?"

"Sure."

Inside her apartment, Amanda said hello to Sassy, put her things on the kitchen bench, grabbed a glass of wine and slumped down into her favourite lounge chair. She was still a bit flustered.

"Hi Phil. What was it about Griffith you wanted to tell me?" She had Phil back on the phone.

"The shooter in your photo has been remanded in custody based on evidence found in his car and at his work." Phil explained.

"That's good."

"Yes, but Tony Pirelli says that Nu Pickers Co-op is a front for a larger criminal organisation, which has its fingers in many criminal activities, not just undocumented migrant workers. He didn't want to scare you, but he did say that you need to be careful. These criminal organisations don't like having their activities disrupted."

"But no one knows about my involvement in the case other than the police." Amanda was starting to get worried.

"That may be true, but you know that things get leaked and how media attention can be hard to resist. So, keep vigilant, call if anything suspicious happens and be careful."

"Ok. Thanks." Amanda was now wondering whether the incident with the car was not really an accident.

The rest of the evening Amanda spent going over what had happened and Tony's warning. She reflected on her visions and how they proved to be helpful but also came with consequences. Did she really want to continue using her phone?

An evening to forget:

The next day went by without anything suspicious occurring. Work was busy, and so far, no one from the media had contacted her about the events in Griffith. That night she was going to dinner with her friends, and when Amanda got home it was all about getting herself ready for what she hoped would be a fun night out.

Amanda was picked up by a ride share service, which took her to St Kilda. Jenni had booked them into Donovan's because she had a hankering for seafood. Both Jenni and Margo were already seated when Amanda arrived.

"Sorry, I'm late again." Amanda warmly embraced her friends before they all resumed their seats.

"No. You're not late. We were early." Jenni suggested with a smile.

"Come on. Tell us all about your latest adventure." Margo came straight to the point. Amanda waited until the waiter had poured them all a glass of wine before she started.

Amanda explained what happened with lots of clarifying questions from her friends. It seemed the evening was all about Amanda's phone and her visions. The food and wine were great and overall, the three friends had a wonderful time enjoying each other's company.

When the three friends left the restaurant, Amanda commented, because it was a beautiful evening, she wanted to stroll along the beach and just chill out. Jenni and Margo had other ideas. They decided to go dancing at a night club in Melbourne and wished Amanda good night, then they headed towards The Esplanade to catch a tram.

Amanda didn't have to go far before she was on the beach. With the sound of the gentle waves and the city lights, she couldn't resist and pulled out her phone. She was going to just take some pictures, but suddenly found herself starting the video. What she saw, on the screen, was totally different to what she was pointing her phone at. Instead of the beach, she was looking at a busy intersection with lots of noise and people walking everywhere. It was still at night, and she could hear the sound through her phone. So, she immediately presumed it was in the future. She didn't have time to look at her watch before a horrific scene unfolded on her phone. A group of people were waiting for the traffic lights to change, she didn't recognise anybody in particular. The lights changed and people started to cross, when suddenly a car came hurtling through the traffic lights, crashing into one woman and knocking her into the air. The video stopped, showing the shock on people's faces, and there was a woman being attended to as she lay motionless on the road.

Amanda was confused. What was the phone trying to tell her? Who was the woman? The snapshot didn't show enough detail and the woman's face was looking away from the camera. Something suddenly made Amanda sick in her stomach. The woman's outfit. Did she recognise it?

Amanda jumped as her phone rang. It was Jenni. Amanda could hardly hear her above the background noise, and she was sobbing.

"Amanda. Amanda. Its Margo. She's been hit."

"What? Where are you?"

"Near Luna Park. She's in a bad way. Come quick."

"I'm coming." Amanda was already running.

By the time Amanda made it to the intersection, Jenni had gone in the ambulance with Margo. Amanda was heartbroken because she hadn't got there in time. She spoke to the police, and they told her which hospital they had taken Margo. She made her way there as quickly as possible and eventually found Jenni, Frank, Margo's husband, and her son Micheal, who had both rushed to the hospital. There were hugs all around. Jenni couldn't hold back her tears. She was witness to the horrific event.

The rest of the night was spent in the hospital waiting room. Scant details were passed on to them by the staff. The police turned up and they heard the distressing news that the driver didn't stop. It was now being treated as a hit-and-run.

The tragic news came mid-morning, the next day. Margo had not made it. Amanda, Jenni, Frank and Micheal did their best to comfort each other. Jenni kept saying, 'What if? She had held Margo back'. Or. 'They had not decided to head into Melbourne via the tram.' Amanda tried to console her. "It's not your fault."

In the back of Amanda's mind, she kept going back to her video and the snapshot she had witnessed through her phone. Could she have done something to prevent Margo's death.

She and Jenni eventually went back to Amanda's apartment, after picking up clothes and a few other things from Jenni's place. They decided to stay together over the next couple of days to look after each other. The pair had been constantly on their phones, as the news filtered through to Margo's huge circle of her friends.

Phil called and offered his condolences. He also offered to keep track of the police investigation and keep them informed. Amanda thanked him, but she didn't mention her vision. She was uncertain as to why she had a vision that ultimately, she could do nothing about. In fact, she was starting to get angry and questioned; '*What is the point of all these visions?*'

Feeling Numb:

Amanda cancelled her training at Tech Corp and the meeting to review her book. She asked Megan to effectively close the office and just field any calls for the next few days. Amanda and Jenni wandered around the apartment like zombies. Only Sassy brought any joy as the days dragged on. Margo's family were organising funeral arrangements and dealing with the police, except that Jenni was obviously a witness. Jenni had to go and give a statement, which didn't help her state of mind.

Amanda kept going back to her vision. It was of the future, but it wasn't clear who was in the accident, plus she had no time to warn anyone. The accident happened virtually within minutes of the vision. It was confusing and frustrating. She couldn't keep it bottled up any longer and eventually told Jenni about the vision of the accident.

Jenni was shocked, confused, and even a bit angry. "Why didn't you warn us?" Amanda did her best to explain that there was no time. The atmosphere between them went a little cold after Amanda's revelation. Jenni hardly said anything, and Amanda felt she needed to do something to climb out of her lethargy.

Amanda got a call from Depindar. She was very sorry to hear about Margo's death. Depindar heard the lethargy in Amanda's voice and suggested that maybe a run would help. Amanda immediately agreed and the next morning they met and went for their usual 5km run.

After their run, Amanda suggested a coffee. They grabbed a takeaway coffee and walked and talked. Amanda hadn't told anyone other than Jenni, Margo, Phil, Megan and her Uncle and Auntie about her visions, today she decided to confide in Depindar. Maybe telling someone else might provide her with a different perspective or even help resolve some of her questions.

Depindar, was non-judgemental, as she listened to Amanda describe why she got her new phone and how the visions manifest themselves in the form of a snapshot at the end of a video. Depindar eventually asked. "How many visions have you had?"

"I've lost count now."

"So, the reunion of the twins, while you were in San Francisco, was because of your visions?" Depindar was starting to put the pieces together as Amanda explained her visions.

"You have visions of the future and of the past?" She asked.

"Yes. Visions of the past didn't happen initially. That's a more recent phenomenon."

"Wow, this is amazing, Amanda, but it must be a bit freaky. Plus, how do you cope with seeing people being shot and …" Depindar stopped talking. She suddenly realised Amanda was softly sobbing. She threw her arm around Amanda's shoulders to console her, as it dawned on her, that may be Amanda had seen Margo's accident.

She quietly asked. "Did you see a vision of the accident?" She didn't want to say Margo's name. Amanda took a moment to compose herself. "Yes. But I couldn't stop it."

They both stopped and stood in silence. Depindar didn't know what to say. Amanda wiped the tears from her eyes. She eventually continued. "It's so frustrating to think I have this gift. I suppose you could call it that, but I have no control over when or how these visions occur. So, what's the point of having them, if I can't act on them to prevent something bad from happening?"

"Sorry, I don't have an answer for you. But maybe if you look at what you have been able to achieve. You can gain some solace. I suppose it's like many things in life. Nothings perfect."

The pair looked at each other and then warmly embraced. "Thanks for being a shoulder to cry on. We had better be heading home. Let's meet for a run tomorrow. I need it as a release mechanism."

"Sure, anytime."

Life goes on

Amanda returned home and told Jenni she had confided with Depindar and as a result felt a little better. She suggested Jenni needed to do something and that moping around the apartment together was not helping them to move on.

Initially, Amanda's suggestion didn't change Jenni's mood. She was in fact now a bit jealous of Amanda. The fact that Amanda had someone else to confide in and that Amanda was already moving on from Margo's death. She brooded for the rest of the morning keeping her distance from Amanda in the confines of the apartment.

By the afternoon, Jenni eventually realised that she was being petty. She came to the conclusion that Amanda was dealing with a lot as a result of her visions. Dwelling on what might have or what might not have happened was not going to resolve things. They were the best of friends and needed each other's support to get on with their lives as best as possible.

Jenni approached Amanda as she was making a coffee in the kitchen.

"I'm sorry. I haven't been at my best. You must be finding it hard to reconcile what happened. I'm here for you. We'll get through this together." The friends gave each other a warm hug.

"That's ok. We will always remember Margo with love and appreciate all the things she meant to us both." Amanda paused then added. "You don't need to worry about Depindar, she will never be a Margo, but she is becoming a good friend."

"I'm not going running." Jenni half smiled.

"No. That's ok. I know that would be a stretch. Cafés and wine bars are more your style."

"Oh. You think you know me? Well, I might surprise you one day." They both had a laugh. Jenni headed for her room. "I'm going to pack and then head home. Work tomorrow."

The friends said their goodbyes. Jenni said she would call tomorrow and then they would see each other at the funeral the next day. Amanda closed the door and looked down at Sassy. "Well, beautiful it's just you and me again." Sassy turned and ran in front of Amanda as she headed back into the apartment.

The funeral was a mixture of sadness and joy. Margo's immediate family where overwhelmed with the outpouring of emotion and support from the huge gathering of friends and associates. Phil Williams was a surprise attendee. Amanda was grateful that he had come to pay his respects.

At the reception later, Phil brought Amanda up to date with the news from Griffith. More incriminating evidence had been found against the shooter. He reiterated that Amanda needed to be careful, and he suggested that he would ask the local police if they could keep an eye on her apartment. Amanda asked if that was really necessary. She felt a bit uncomfortable having people watch over her.

Phil insisted that it was a worthwhile precaution. Amanda reluctantly agreed.

Slowly over the next week, life started to get back to normal. Amanda started her training sessions at Tech Corp, and she renegotiated a book review with her publisher. Working with the publisher without Margo felt odd and was a reminder of her loss.

Phil kept in contact to make sure Amanda remained vigilant. Amanda also decided to bring Megan fully into her confidence and tell her everything. Megan had some idea of Amanda's visions but when she heard about the vision of Margo's accident, she was shocked.

"That must have been horrible. I'm so sorry. I had no idea you were coping with that vision and Margo's death."

"Thank you. I'm getting better at dealing with it." Amanda was grateful for Megan's support.

"Oh my god. And all this on top of the Griffith shooting. You're amazing."

"I wouldn't go that far." Amanda laughed. "Still, dealing with and trying to understand these visions is a challenge."

"Certainly, I'm here to help and I'm sure your close friends are supportive as well." Megan gave Amanda a warm smile.

Tragedy strikes twice

On her way home that night, Amanda had that unnerving feeling again, that she was being watched or that someone was following her. She wondered if Phil had arranged for the police to have someone to tail her. Once in her apartment she rang Phil to ask him. "Hi Amanda. How are you faring?"

"Fine thanks. Things are getting better. I called to ask you about my police protection. Did you ask them to follow me?"

"No. That's not usual practice. I only asked as a favour, if they could regularly send someone past your apartment just to see if anyone suspicious were lurking about. They didn't actually say that they would do it. Why, has something happened?"

"I maybe a bit paranoid at the moment but I am getting a sense that someone might be following me."

"Really. Don't dismiss those feelings of yours. You know you are a psychic." Phil added the last bit to get a reaction.

"Oh, come on. You know I don't think of myself as a psychic. It's more my phone."

"You keep saying that. Is there any way one of your close friends could accompany you to and from work for the next few days. Another set of eyes could be helpful." Phil suggested.

Amanda started thinking of options. "I suppose it wouldn't hurt to ask. Alright, I'll let you know how things go. Bye." Amanda immediately thought of Depindar. She lived nearby and worked mostly from home. *'I'll bring it up tomorrow during our run.'*

She hoped Depindar would agree and went to bed feeling a little more at ease.

"Of course. No problems." Depindar agreed straight away. "I'll come to your place, and we can go for our run from there. Then I'll go home shower and come back to be your escort. At night, just give me a call half an hour before you decide to leave, and I'll come get you."

"Sounds great. I've decided to work from home a few more days a week in the short term. So, you'll only need to get me from work, one or two days a week." Amanda was feeling grateful and reassured by Depindar's support.

They had finished their run and were walking back to Amanda's apartment. The pair had not noticed a car slowly moving behind them. Suddenly, they heard wheels scream as the car sped up. The passenger side window came down and there was a single shot.

Everything seemed to happen in slow motion. Above the sound of a woman screaming, Amanda's phone could be heard ringing. A fumbling hand grabbed it out of the pouch on her arm. The other hand was applying pressure to a head wound trying to stem the blood flow.

A male voice asked. "Hello Amanda? What's happened?"

"She's been shot."

"Who is that?"

"Depindar. Amanda's been shot. I need help." Depindar started yelling. "Help! Help! Call an ambulance." To anybody that could hear.

"I'm on it." Phil replied, but Depindar didn't hear. She had placed the phone ground, so she could apply her other hand to Amanda's head wound. People started to gather around the two women. Some asked what they could do to help. Depindar kept asking. "Where's the ambulance?" As she continued to apply pressure to Amanda's head wound. Her blood seemed to be everywhere.

The ambulance was there in a matter of minutes. The police had also arrived in force. They quickly cordoned off the area and moved the onlookers back. Depindar went in the ambulance with Amanda. She made sure she collected Amanda's phone. She checked that it wasn't damaged and then called Phil back.

"We're on our way to the hospital. She has lost a lot of blood." Depindar's voice was trembling.

"Thanks for the call. I'm on the next flight down." He didn't want to press Depindar for detail on what had happened. There would be time later for that. Next Depindar found Jenni's number and called her.

"Hi Amanda. What's up?" Jenni suddenly registered that an ambulance siren was blaring in the background.

"Jenni. This is Depindar. Amanda's been shot." There was a gasp on the other end of the phone. Time seemed to stand still. The ambulance siren filling the void.

"Oh my god!" Jenni finally responded. "What happened? Where are you?" The questions came thick and fast.

Depindar kept it brief. Just enough details to placate Jenni for now. She had found out that the ambulance was heading for The Alfred Hospital in Commercial Road. Jenni said she would meet them there and then ended the call.

At the emergency entrance, Amanda was rushed further into the hospital, presumably for immediate surgery. Depindar was ushered into a triage room to be checked over. She was covered in blood and the emergency staff wanted to see if she might also have been wounded. Luckily, Depindar had no visible injuries. The hospital staff continually reassured Depindar that Amanda was in good hands and that everything was being done to help her.

It wasn't long before some police showed up. Depindar was wearing a hospital gown by then and was sitting quietly on a bed. Two officers got a quick statement from Depindar, checked that she was uninjured and then a female constable was assigned the sit with Depindar until detectives came to conduct a formal interview.

Jenni arrived with Amanda's parents, Tom and Stella. After quick introductions, Amanda's parents were ushered away by one of the doctors. Amanda's life was in the balance. Jenni remained in the room with Depindar, and they nervously chatted. Asking each other questions about what they did. Where they lived. Avoiding the matter of Amanda's condition.

Phil Williams arrived after lunch. He initially spent time with the police, gleaning as much information as he could about the shooting. He briefed the police on the events that occurred in Griffith and the possibility of criminal gang involvement. They were surprised and queried him about his role. Phil kept it as vague as possible. He then spent time with Depindar going over the incident as sympathetically as he could. He also looked at Amanda's phone. She had given him the pin to open the phone some time ago. It looked just like a normal phone. He opened the AFP tracking app, wondering how the phone activated the alarm without Amanda doing anything. It was the third time it had happened, which was unnerving.

Amanda underwent a couple of operations. The bullet had luckily passed through her head without causing major damage. Only minor fracturing. Doctors had to remove small fragments of Amanda's skull and were optimistic that she would not suffer major brain damage. However, she was still in a critical condition and would be in the intensive care unit (ICU) for a couple of days. Phil couldn't stay, eventually saying his goodbyes, and returned to Canberra. With Amanda in ICU, her parents invited both Jenni and Depindar to use their house as a meeting place, while everyone waited to see how Amanda faired.

Jenni and Depindar grew closer together over the following days as they waited. On the fourth day after the shooting, they arrived at

Amanda's parents' house, and there was good news. Amanda had been moved out of ICU and they could now visit her in hospital. She was still in a coma and had a long way to go.

Hospital vigil

Tom and Stella, Jenni and Depindar decided to take turns in sitting with Amanda while they waited for her to recover. That way Jenni and Depindar could return to work. Depindar took the early morning shift. Amanda's father took over before lunch. Jenni came after work and stayed late, until Amanda's mum relieved her after midnight. Phil called every day to get an update on Amanda's condition and he passed on any information he could from the police investigation.

Amanda's condition didn't seem to be changing. The doctors had hoped she would have come out of her coma by now and everybody was starting to fear for the worst.

Jenni was sitting next to Amanda's bed, holding her hand. The doctors had reported that all her vital signs were good. However, she wasn't out of danger yet; they would have to see how she responded as they attempted to bring her out of the coma. Also, there was still no way of knowing if she had suffered any permanent brain damage, whilst still in the coma.

Jenni was depressed and began to sob as she thought about losing her best friend. "Please, Amanda don't leave me. I don't know if I can cope with losing both you and Margo."

That day, Amanda's phone had somehow found its way into Amanda's other hand, which lay across her lap. Jenni suddenly noticed it flashed and then the screen came on its own. She was a little unnerved when a video started playing. She moved closer to get a good look. The video showed the back of Jenni's car. It had stopped, in what Jenni thought was Amanda's Street. Jenni saw herself get out of her car and walk around to the passenger's side. She opened the door and helped Amanda gingerly step out of the car. Jenni couldn't believe that she was hearing herself. "Careful Amanda, watch your step, you're nearly home."

In the video, Amanda gave Jenni a warm embrace. She was now facing the camera, smiled and spoke to her. "Thank you."

The video stopped with a snapshot of the friends embracing. Jenni smiled with joy and let out a big sigh of relief as she lowered her head onto Amanda's shoulder. "Looks like all will be ok."

To Jenni's surprise, she felt Amanda's other hand stroke her hair. Then Amanda spoke, "I know. By the way, Margo says she will always be with us."